To Bobbie,

Peace and Joy be with you,

Like a Fig Tree

Judy Mitchell Rich

Judy Mitchell Rich

Copyright © 2015 Judy Mitchell Rich
www.judymitchellrich.com

Please protect writers and other creative people by taking the legal statement seriously: All legal rights reserved. No portion of the book may be reproduced, stored in a retrieval system, or transmitted in any form or by any means— electronic, mechanical, photocopy, recording, scanning, or other—except for brief quotations in critical reviews or articles, without the prior written permission of the publisher.

This book is a work of fiction. All the characters, dialogue, plot and resolution are products of the author's imagination. Any resemblance to persons living or dead is entirely coincidental, and any real settings are used fictitiously.

Verses quoted from the King James Version of the Bible are noted as such. All other Scripture quotations contained herein are from the New Revised Standard Version Bible, copyright © 1989, by the Division of Christian Education of the National Council of the Churches of Christ in the U.S.A.

Typesetting and cover design by FormattingExperts.com
Cover picture used by permission of LegendsOfAmerica.com
Author's photo by Shane Hunter Photography, Huntsville, Alabama

Also by Judy Mitchell Rich

Like Sheep
Like a Fox

Contents

Acknowledgements 7

Chapter 1 15

Chapter 2 19

Chapter 3 25

Chapter 4 31

Chapter 5 37

Chapter 6 43

Chapter 7 47

Chapter 8 57

Chapter 9 69

Chapter 10 75

Chapter 11 83

Chapter 12 93

Chapter 13 97

Chapter 14 107

Chapter 15 111

Chapter 16 115

Chapter 17 123

Chapter 18 127

Chapter 19 137

Chapter 20 145

Chapter 21 151

Chapter 22 161

Chapter 23 173

Chapter 24 177

Chapter 25 185

Chapter 26 189

Chapter 27 201

Acknowledgements

Thanks to friends and family members who read and reread this novel, giving feedback, advice, and encouragement: my sons Matt Todd and Mitch Todd; Houston Hodges; writer's group members, John Bush, Joyce Pettis, and Peggy Towns. Thank you to frequent advisors and supporters: sisters Susan Bryan, Rebecca Cartier, Sally Mitchell, Kate Murray; and friends Brenda Cash, and Betty Brown. My appreciation to wise women from whom I've learned much, Loretta Ross and Margaret Haney. Special thanks to the Rev. Jan Todd whose experience with the searchlight is used with her permission. The Revs. Mitch and Jan Todd gave me a grand tour of Wichita, and the Rev. Shannon Webster generously shared information about Wichita. Thanks to all of you for supporting my writing habit.

For the Rev. Jan E. Todd

In the morning as they passed by, they saw the fig tree withered away to its roots. Then Peter remembered and said to him, "Rabbi, look! The fig tree that you cursed has withered."

Jesus answered them, "Have faith in God. Truly I tell you, if you say to this mountain, 'Be taken up and thrown into the sea,' and if you do not doubt in your heart, but believe that what you say will come to pass, it will be done for you."

Mark 11:20-23 NRSV

1992

WICHITA, KANSAS

Chapter 1

Two women in the second row clasped the back of the pew, pulled themselves up, and glared. The older woman waited in the aisle until the younger one joined her, and they slowly made their way to the rear, chins held high, hair pulled into identical buns, and backsides swaying like huge balloons.

Suzanne stumbled over her words, and waited to continue her sermon until they reached the back of the sanctuary. They turned their heads in unison and looked back at the congregation. The older woman smirked as they joined hands and marched out the door.

Great, Suzanne thought. Trouble already. If this wasn't my first Sunday, I'd be worried about what I'd done to upset them. I may have said yes to this position too quickly. Do I really want to take on another troubled congregation? She looked around. All eyes were on her. Don't think about it now, she told herself. Get on with worship. No doubt Dave will fill you in after church. The one-man welcome committee had already given her more information than she could retain.

She repeated her last point. "You and I have been brought together in God's timing so we can let the good news shine in this time and place. I'll be your interim pastor for a while, and in that time we'll try to discern God's will for your future. There's an adventure ahead of us."

A young man in the front row looked up, eyes locked on hers, his face open and hungry. Other eyes stared and waited. *O God,* she prayed silently, *I haven't a clue what they need.* She'd only had three days to prepare for this Sunday, an emergency, she'd been told. Their pastor had been forced to resign.

After the sermon a man with a gray ponytail came forward with his guitar. He played and sang "Jesus Walked this Lonesome Valley" like he'd been in that valley. I have much to learn about these people, she thought, but they won't be strangers for long.

The presbytery committee spokesperson, who had asked her to be the interim pastor for Lamb of God Presbyterian Church in Wichita, had cryptically filled her in on their situation: "Mostly blue collar workers, former pastor still in the community, he started several Alcoholics Anonymous groups, been there seventeen years, health failing. You'll be needed for one to two years to help them prepare for new leadership."

The call came at a good time for her. She dreaded the looming empty nest. In the fall Peter would begin college, and Julie already talked about nothing but KU, even though she still had her senior year in high school ahead of her. Suzanne had stayed home with them since Peter suffered a head injury during her previous interim. She had watched over him like a hawk, limiting his activities to prevent another injury.

She hadn't exactly regretted filling her days with home, school and children; however, the call to be a pastor had never gone away. An empty hole in her chest begged to be filled. On the other hand, for that three and a half years the whole family attended the same church like they had in Columbus. This time it was Bell's church. And she took an active role as the pastor's spouse, teaching the kindergarten Sunday School class, making calls with Bell—he hated making calls on people—and tending to details for him—he was terrible at dealing with mail, taking care of paperwork, and keeping a calendar. Most people didn't know that. His congregation loved that he moved around the sanctuary while he preached and didn't use notes. And he had made a name for himself when he began an organization for the churches in town to coordinate their assistance with food, clothing and transportation for those in need. He was good at that. She freed him up to do that important work.

Peter and Julie's high school activities in music and drama kept the whole family busy. And their joys and traumas of dating ruled the family's emotional climate. Suzanne admitted to herself that she had lived vicariously through her children the last few years. She and Bell enjoyed helping with costumes and sets for their plays and musicals. But now that Peter and Julie's eyes were focused on colleges and future plans, it was time for her to step back. Any time she tried to discuss decisions he was making, Peter circled his arms overhead to imitate the hovering of a helicopter.

He had decided to follow his on again-off again girlfriend Amy to Southwestern College in Winfield, Kansas. Suzanne wanted him to be logical about it, but he couldn't be logical with Amy in the equation. *I shouldn't complain*, she reminded herself often. *They offered him a full scholarship.*

Julie was intent on going to the University of Kansas in Lawrence, but when asked why, she would only grin and say she liked the Jayhawk mascot. Her father tried to get her to talk about what she was going to study and why KU, but Suzanne assured him Julie would reveal her reasons when she was ready. Bell shook his head, "She's not thinking clearly about this. I don't understand." *Of course, you don't*, Suzanne thought. *That's why she won't tell you. She saw how you reacted to Peter following Amy, so she knows you won't approve of her choosing KU because Matthew is going there.*

He didn't exactly approve of Suzanne going back to being a church pastor either. "It's too far away," he said. "It's another floundering church that won't take advantage of your abilities.

The pay is way too low." They were the same arguments as always. She suspected they stemmed from feelings of guilt. Seven years earlier shehad left a thriving parish in Columbus so he could move from being Director of Social Services back to the parish ministry. He was offered the position of pastor of a large Presbyterian church in Salina. The only opening available for her back then was as an interim pastor for a tiny church which sat in the wheat fields near Salina. After that year, she served another congregation as an interim, and now here she was taking on one in Wichita, an hour and a half away from home.

But the drive is easy, she told herself, all interstate until I leave it on the northern edge of the city limits. Then it's only ten minutes to the church.

* * *

On her first trip to the church, she'd felt a wave of foreboding when she passed an acre of dead, scavenged school buses across the road from a warehouse parking lot, which held a gazillion UPS trucks. Then there were huge expanses of farming equipment and semi cabs. Nearer to her destination, there were vacant weedy lots. She passed an overgrown cemetery next to a church which had a for sale sign out front. A tire store sat next to a closed motel. One house had junk and garbage covering the yard from front door to street. It looked as though the people opened the door and threw out what they didn't want. Maybe they came from an area that didn't have garbage service, she thought.

Finally, she arrived at the church. It sat on the corner of two roads that to the south and east serviced businesses. But the neighborhood around the church which was north of the city of Wichita and west near the levee had seen better days. Yards held more dirt than weeds, and most of the cottages needed paint. Another challenge, another culture I've never experienced, she thought.

Chapter 2

Suzanne stood by the front door of the sanctuary and shook hands. "Welcome, Pastor," "Nice sermon," "Mornin'." When all had exited the sanctuary and moved toward the basement for refreshments, she sighed with relief and walked back toward the pulpit to pick up her papers. First Sundays were always a challenge.

The room depressed her. Windows were covered with film intended to look like stained glass. The wooden floor looked permanently dirty, and dust balls collected under the pews. Behind those six pews sat four rows of scratched up theater seats attached at the arms. Their thin, cracked seats folded up.

A cross, backlit by fluorescent lights, hung on the front wall behind a small platform and its central pulpit. Choir chairs crowded together on both sides and faced the pulpit. It was a little claustrophobic for her taste.

The people were quite attentive, she thought. I wonder what they took away with them. I pray the Spirit spoke. It will take me a while to know the best ways to communicate. However, I'll probably find salt of the earth people here, as I have in every church, and the sanctuary will become a sacred space for me. Maybe.

Stop being negative, she told herself. Get downstairs and concentrate on the people. Once you know them, the atmosphere will change for you.

* * *

She entered the crowded basement and snaked around the tables to get to her office. After emptying her arms and hanging her robe in the closet, she moved back out into the midst of lively chatter. Signs of a healthy church, she thought, people stay to visit, and the talk sounds happy. The smell of coffee and the sound of a man laughing under his breath took her back to after-church fellowships when she was young. Of course, at an Air Force base chapel, the men and women dressed in uniform, or sometimes the women wore high heels and dresses. God forbid anyone would wear torn jeans that showed her underwear like the woman in front of her, who rocked from one foot to the other as she loaded her plate with refreshments.

I don't need to worry about I wear here, Suzanne thought, as she looked around. In fact, I may look a little stuffy to them. She wore a red suit, and in order to look as tall as she could, she'd pulled her long, blond hair up into a chignon on top of her head.

Dave's wife Eileen fussed with dishes on a long table full of food. "Pastor Suzanne, come have something to eat," Eileen said. "We have little egg muffins here and fruit. Down a little further you'll find coffee cake, banana bread, and cookies." Eileen's two front teeth stuck out so far her mouth hardly closed around them, and when she tried to smile, it turned into a grimace, but her eyes crinkled with joy.

"Eileen, thank you. It's quite a spread. Did you make all this?"

Her eyes lit up. "Yes, I guess I'm the church cook. These young people don't eat well, you know."

"She helps us keep up our strength." Her husband interrupted with a big smile. "Pastor, I'd like you to meet Gerald Rains. This is his first time here. We were together last week and I invited him." Suzanne stood as tall as she could, but Dave towered over all of them.

"Gerald," she said shaking his hand. "Welcome. I'm as new

as you are, but I have a sneaky suspicion Dave here knows the answers to any questions either of us might have. Do you live in the area?"

The man's leathery face sank further back into itself and the trembling she had noticed around his chin increased. What can I say to relieve his anxiety? she wondered.

Dave said, "Gerald has lived around here all his life. We've run into each other a time or two over the years. Hey, there's somebody else I want you to meet," he said to the poor man, dragging him off to a small group near the coffee pot.

Suzanne's feet hurt. She was ready to go home long before people headed for their cars.

She helped Dave and Eileen carry dishes to the kitchen, wondering when someone would tell her about the two women who walked out. Finally, she and Dave were alone in the kitchen. He washed dishes and she dried them. "Dave, who were the two women who left church?"

His forehead wrinkled, but then his head jerked up. "Oh, oh, yes." He looked around. "Let's talk about that another time."

* * *

Suzanne's spirits drooped on the long drive home. Dull, flat fields provided no distraction. The few cattle she saw stared at the ground. Boredom, nothing but boredom all the way to the horizon. Even the occasional oil pumps looked lonely, sitting in the midst of scrubby grass.

By now the wheat will be beautiful in some places, she thought. It's spring. There should be signs of life everywhere. I wonder if they don't get much rain in this part of the state. All I can see is dullness everywhere. But it could be that I'm dull. Maybe I'm not ready to go back to work. Yet, when they asked me, I felt an electrical charge run from the bottom of my stomach all the way to my heart. Is that enough to indicate a call from God? Perhaps it's simply a call from my ego. If I hadn't jumped to accept the challenge of this church, I could be enjoying the last months with Peter at home instead of leaving him before he can leave me. A sob escaped her throat before she knew it was coming.

* * *

Finally home, she heard the phone ringing before she opened the door from the garage to the kitchen, and she dashed to answer it.

"Suzanne?" her mother said.

"Mother, is anything wrong?"

"No, why would you think that?"

"You don't usually call on Sundays since we're at church."

"Oh, yes, I forgot it was Sunday. You're at a new church, aren't you? I'm surprised you went back to doing that."

"Just a second, let me go to the phone in the family room. Hang on. I'll leave this one off the hook so we don't lose our connection." She slipped off her shoes and moved to her overstuffed chair. "Now then, Mom, tell me, how are things in Alabama?"

"Good, real good. Of course, it seems like most of our time is spent going to doctors. Life is one appointment after another. How are Peter and Julie?"

"They're fine, still at church with Bell. The youth had a dinner today. They're excited about prom next Saturday. And last week was Godspell. They both sang in the chorus. I wish you could have been here."

"You know, it's impossible to get your father to go anywhere."

"Yes, Mom, I know. I'm glad you called. There's something I've been wanting to ask you. I'm really sad about Peter leaving for college and then Julie going off next year. Did you feel that way when we went off to school?"

"Suzanne, sweetheart, you are so sensitive, always have been. To me it was the most natural thing in the world for you girls to go off on your own."

Suzanne fell silent while her mother rambled on. Why did I think she would understand? She never has. Maybe she didn't love us the way I love Peter and Julie. But everyone loves a little differently. Her perfectionism for herself and us girls may have kept us from feeling her kind of love. And then Dad .... With his temper and rages, it was hard to trust his. I hope Melanie, Elizabeth and Rebecca felt the love more than I did. At least wherever we moved I was able to take them to church. It was peaceful there, almost like a second family.

Ten minutes later, she hung up and went looking for something to eat. A pizza box on the kitchen table held a small dry triangle, a sure sign that last night's leftover pizza had been breakfast for Peter and Julie. She settled for crackers and cheese. The house felt cold, the quiet felt heavy.

Chapter 3

On Monday morning, Suzanne lugged a box of books into the side door of the church and down the stairs to the basement. "You must be Melba," Suzanne said as she set the box on one of the long tables.

"That's me." The thin, angular woman leaned against her office door, arms crossed. The phone rang, and she darted into her office while Suzanne continued unloading her car.

She moved boxes to the scarred and battered wood desk provided for her. It backed up against the outside concrete block wall under a high rectangular window. From the desk chair she could see across the main room to the secretary's desk. Melba perched there talking on the phone. The whole time Suzanne carried boxes in and set up her office, Melba talked. It sounded like her apartment manager wasn't taking her lack of hot water seriously.

It didn't take long to unpack. She put her books on upper and lower shelves and pictures of her family at eye level. In one of them Peter, Julie, and Bell smiled proudly at an honors assembly when Peter was named valedictorian. In another the four of them—plus her parents, sisters and their families—were all dressed in red at their Christmas gathering in Alabama.

She hung pictures of the four churches she'd served: First, the large brick church in a Chicago suburb where she'd been a co-associate with Bell; second, a neighborhood church in Columbus,

Ohio. She'd served there as a solo pastor and still grieved over leaving it. The other two photographs showed Harvest and Middletown churches in Kansas. She'd been an interim pastor for each of them. The pictures brought back warm memories of people who made up her great big, wide-spread church family.

Finally, Melba hung up the phone and sat down at her desk. She didn't look up when Suzanne stood at her door and not even when she said, "Melba, let's take a few minutes to get acquainted."

"Sure. What do you want to know?" she said putting on her glasses, picking up a pencil and staring at her notepad.

Suzanne sat down across the desk from her. "Tell me, what is your usual routine?"

"What do you mean?" She paused with pencil hanging in mid-air, still not looking up.

"I see your office hours are nine to three Monday through Friday. I'm used to having the Sunday service material ready by Wednesday noon and then proofreading the bulletin by Thursday noon. How does that work for you?"

"Fine."

"Okay. And the newsletter. Do you publish one every month?"

"July and August are combined."

"I will have articles to you ten days before the end of the month so you can have it finished and mailed by the last day of the month."

Melba stared, for the first time looking her in the eyes.

"Is that enough time for you?"

"Maybe."

Suzanne looked around. "No computer?"

"I'll never use one of those things. If you want things done on a fancy machine, you'll have to get a new secretary."

"So you use a typewriter?"

"Yes. Then I make copies. We keep the copier next door in the parsonage. That's to control who uses it."

"I'll take care of moving it over here. Let's see." Suzanne checked her notes. "How do you answer the phone?"

"'Lamb of God Presbyterian Church. This is Melba.'"

"Fine. I'd like you to use the intercom to let me know I have a call unless I'm with someone. Of course, if it's an emergency, please interrupt me."

"I've never used the intercom, don't know if it works."

"If my door's closed, how would you let me know if it's an emergency?"

"I always yelled, 'Norm, emergency call.' You can hear through these walls—they're pretty thin."

"Can you overhear conversations in my office if the door is closed?"

"If it's a man I can sometimes—but I never gossip. I never tell anything I hear."

"Good, that's important. I guess you'll have to knock on my door if I'm needed. And I'll put a radio out here on one of these tables between your office and mine so that no one will be overheard if they're talking about confidential matters. How about that? We can take turns choosing the station."

"Are you going to make a lot of changes, 'cause that's not going to go over well with these people. Norm always ran things by me. I could tell him how people would respond. You can trust me with confidential matters. And I know a lot about these people if you want to know anything." She twirled her pencil like a baton, around each finger one way and then the opposite, talking the whole time. "I took care of whatever Pastor Norm needed. Brenda—that's his wife—didn't have time. We've always helped each other out. One time before a funeral his robe was so wrinkled I couldn't stand for him to be seen in it. I dashed home to press it."

The door at the top of the stairs banged shut. Saved by the bell, Suzanne thought, as Dave stepped heavily down the stairs and into the room. His eyes darted to Melba and then to Suzanne. She hurriedly moved to lead him to her office. "Dave, come in, sit down. Cup of tea, coffee?"

He shook his head, quickly removed his Royals cap and pounded it with his fist as though it were a baseball glove. Suzanne closed her office door and motioned him to a chair. "I'm glad you came by. Finally, I can stop guessing why those two women left during the worship service yesterday."

"Yes." He cleared his throat and whispered, "They um, well, they didn't say anything to me. But I can tell you the older one is Norm's wife Brenda. You know, Norm Carrollton was our pastor. The younger one is their daughter Pat."

"Hmmm," Suzanne said. "How strange that they would get up and leave like that. I guess I need to visit them and see what more I can learn. Will you go with me?"

"No, no," Dave said, his eyes wide. "I don't think you wanna go and do that."

"Why? Tell me more."

"Norm didn't want to stop preaching, see, and Brenda and Pat are real mad. It'll be a cold day in hell before they accept anybody else in that pulpit. The Presbytery folks told Norm to stay away from the church. It's not very Christian of me, but I think they shoulda told Brenda and Pat that, too." He stood up. "I gotta go. Eileen's waiting in the truck."

Suzanne walked out with him, and they stood by Eileen's open window. She sat in the pickup with her arms crossed and lips pursed around those prominent teeth. "Eileen, how are you this morning?" Suzanne asked with all the cheer she could muster. Getting a gruff "Fine," in response, she went on. "I'm glad to see you. There are some things about this church I need to find out, like who the members are and the names of any who are in nursing homes or hospitals. Would you two help me get started, maybe go visit people with me?"

Dave had already given her details about the worship service, the building and dates for meetings coming up, but that was all framework. Now she needed to get acquainted with people.

Eileen's eyes blazed. "I don't drive. My baking keeps me pretty busy. Anyway, I do enough for this church."

They both turned to Dave. He put his cap on and looked off down the street.

Suzanne waited. She had learned not to ask a man to spend time with her unless she included his wife in the conversation.

Dave said, "Sure. I can do that. Right now I'm working nights, so it would have to be in the late afternoon."

"Best not to make a big deal out of this," Eileen said, her arms still crossed tightly over her bosom. "People get jealous if anyone's shown favoritism."

Dave took a deep breath. "Somebody spray painted all over our house last night," he said to Suzanne.

"Why would anyone do that?" Suzanne asked.

"Humph," Eileen said, "I can guess."

Chapter 4

Later that week on Friday evening, Suzanne waited in the church basement for the elders to gather for a Session meeting. She had given up part of her day off since it was the only evening Dave could meet.

Ten minutes early a woman slowly and carefully descended the basement stairs on four inch heels. She looked like an older version of Dolly Parton with a prominent bosom, big hair, and skin tight jeans.

"Pastor Suzanne, sorry I missed your first Sunday. Mama was sick." She grinned broadly and spoke with a lilting country twang, a lot like Dolly's. "But here I am, and we're tickled pink that you're here. I'm Loretta."

The door slammed, and Dave jogged down the steps followed by Melba. "The sky opened up and there's hail and lightning like I haven't seen in a month of Sundays," Dave said. "It'll probably keep some elders home tonight. May won't come out in this. That's for sure. She's on the other side of Flat Road. It always floods. Jim and Marvin called. They have a regular meeting on Fridays, and they had to go. But we won't have to meet on Friday night again on account of me. I'll be off this schedule soon."

Loretta turned to Suzanne, "Pat is the other elder on the session. That's Norm's daughter. I don't know if she'll come."

"Hey, Loretta," Melba said. "I heard you on the radio today."

Loretta's face brightened. "You did? What song was it?"

Melba sang in her cracked voice, "His eye is on the sparrow and I know he watches me."

"One of my favorites," Loretta said. "Grand Mama sings it all the time."

"Pastor Suzanne," Dave said, "have you met Loretta's grandmother yet?"

"No, I haven't."

"She's another Suzanne and a wise woman of God."

Loretta beamed. "We'll have you over to meet her and Mama one day soon when they're both feeling well enough for visitors. Grand Mama is ninety-two now and a delight to live with. Say, Dave, I hear somebody painted ugliness on your house."

"Do you have any idea why someone would do that?" Suzanne asked.

He shrugged. "Eileen's furious. They painted 'AA' all over the front porch and four letter words on the rest."

"Who do you think it was?" Melba asked.

"Not a clue."

"AA—Alcoholics Anonymous?" Suzanne asked.

Dave nodded. "It certainly wouldn't be anyone in our AA groups."

"But it has to be someone who knows what AA stands for," Loretta said. "What an ignorant thing to do."

"Ignorant and cruel," Suzanne said. She motioned to the table where she had laid out an agenda for the meeting at six places. "Let's sit down. Melba, are you on the Session?"

"I always come to report on the finances," she said claiming a place at the head of the table.

"That coffee smells good, and I think it's ready." Suzanne said. "I'll get us some while we wait a few more minutes." She called to them from the kitchen, "What's a quorum for you?" No one knew.

They sipped coffee and sat looking at each other. Suzanne

picked up the agenda, "Let's see if there are any matters we can deal with while we wait. Melba, let's put you first so you can go on home. Do you have financial reports to hand out?"

"No, I didn't print a new one since we're in the middle of the month, but we're doing fine."

Suzanne stifled her impulse to react and instead asked, "Don't you usually have session meetings this week of the month?"

"Yes," Melba said, "but you being so new and all, I wasn't sure ...." Her voice trailed off.

"What do you suggest?" Suzanne asked the group.

"Let's wait 'til next month," Loretta said.

Dave nodded.

"Okay, Melba. Thank you for coming. We'll wait until next month's meeting to review our income and expenses. Please make me a copy of the budget and your last report when you come in on Monday. It sounds like the rain has let up, so we'll let you go on home to get dry and warm."

"It was hardly worth coming," Melba muttered.

Suzanne looked to see how the other two responded, wondering if she had been too curt with Melba. Their stoic faces gave her no clue. She had a feeling she had tripped over something. She never knew what local custom she'd break. In one place it's understood that meetings start on time and are quickly dispensed with so everyone can get home early; in another, meetings are social events, slow, meandering, and filled with laughter. No matter how careful she was or how lightly she tread, she always fell flat on her face about something in the early weeks at a church.

She proceeded in her preferred style: get the work done and go home. Neither Dave nor Loretta had a copy of the bylaws. They'd never seen any personnel policies and had no opinion about what days she took off.

"I don't think Norm had any certain day off," Loretta said.

* * *

Suzanne drove through the dark wet roads and onto the interstate. Loretta and Dave will be home by eight, she thought. It'll take me until nine or nine-thirty. I guess the kids will be at school decorating for the prom.

* * *

Squeals of laughter and footsteps clomping on the stairs woke Suzanne on Saturday morning. "Sarah and Matthew are here," Bell mumbled and rolled over.

Suzanne met them in the kitchen. "Look at you two. You're so grown up. All four of you are."

"MamaSuze, good morning," Sarah hugged her. "Guess what! I'm going to the prom with Peter."

Her brother Matthew gave Suzanne a half hug. "And I'm going with Julie." They all laughed. That was no surprise. Matthew and Julie had been dating for two years. But Peter's date was supposed to be Amy. Probably having one of her "moods," Suzanne thought. That girl had broken up with Peter several times, even throwing his class ring at him the last time, then a week later crying to him that she didn't mean it. Amy didn't fit Suzanne's idea of a good partner for Peter, but Sarah—Sarah Edwards would be a dream come true.

Matthew and Sarah, their older brother Robert, and their parents had been close friends of the whole family since Suzanne's interim pastorate at Covenant Church in Middletown. The families still vacationed together a couple of times a year at the Edwards' cabin on Marion Lake. The boys were the same age and their sisters were not only born the same year but also on the same day. When they first met, the girls were eleven and the boys twelve. She had watched them grow into young men and women. Their mother Jewell had become a trusted friend to Suzanne. Their father Ed and older brother Robert kept everyone laughing when they were together. And Bell liked talked fishing and sports with Ed.

Manicures, corsages, hairdos. Suzanne fixed both girls' hair and helped with their makeup. Bell helped the boys with their tuxes then disappeared and returned home with a cream colored Bonneville convertible that he had rented for the evening. Loud music and laughter filled the house. And there were pictures, lots of pictures taken. Ed had toted all his professional equipment for what he called "an official photo shoot." That lasted until the four insisted they had to leave and finally drove off.

"Come on, Suzanne and Bell," Ed said. "We're taking you old people out to dinner."

Chapter 5

The next week on a Tuesday afternoon Suzanne walked across the side yard of the church to the house next door. It was one of a dozen small tract houses in the neighborhood, most of them like this one, dirty white with weedy yards. She knocked on the aluminum screen door. The center of it held a curly C for Carrollton. She hadn't told anyone she intended to visit the former pastor. In fact Melba had told her he lived next door and warned her not to go near there. However, this seemed to Suzanne the best place to start trying to relieve the tension surrounding him and his leaving. *I need to get someone to carry that copier back to the church, too,* she reminded herself. *I'll call Dave this afternoon.* She squared her shoulders ready to face his wife and daughter, who clearly did not want her in the pulpit. They had continued to walk out each time the sermon began. However, the previous Sunday when they stood up, scowled in unison, and walked out, hardly anyone looked at them. Others had arrived early and filled in the front pews, so the two had to sit about half way back.

***

Suzanne waited, wondering if she should knock again. *If no one's there, it won't matter if I do,* she reasoned. After a louder knock, several minutes went by, and she turned to leave. But the door opened. The unshaven man wore a crisp white shirt, a navy suit and red tie. A huge silver cross hung on his chest.

"Reverend Carrollton, I'm Suzanne Hawkins, the interim pastor at Lamb of God. Could we talk a few minutes?"

He opened the door wide but said nothing. She walked in. He still stood at the door. "Shall we sit in here?" she asked pointing to the living room, but her smile and question met with a stare and silence.

After a long, awkward pause, she sat down on the closest chair. He closed the door and then sat on the couch opposite her. Behind him calendar pictures of cats hung crooked, thumbtacked on the wall. A real tabby cat pranced in and rubbed against Suzanne's ankles. That explained the odor in the house.

"Norm, I wanted to meet you and establish a good connection," she said. "So often previous pastors and new ones feel competition and resentment. I don't want that to happen. I hope to build on all the good you've done here."

"Thank you."

Where do I go from here? Suzanne wondered. I don't want to ask about the rudeness of his wife and daughter, but I'd like to know his feelings. "Your wife and daughter have been in church, but I haven't had a chance to talk with them. They've left early."

Nothing. No smile, no frown. Not even a grunt. He simply stared at her with blank eyes.

"Are they here?" she asked.

He shook his head.

"Is there anything you'd like to tell me about the church?"

He cleared his throat and spoke in a preacherly voice. "I came here in '75. Lots of trouble with alcohol in the neighborhood. Started Alcoholics Anonymous groups. They're good people." He spoke as though his words had been repeated many times.

"That sounds like a great legacy."

His eyebrows moved together and his mouth curved down. His

chest caved in and he looked at the floor.

I have to get out of here, Suzanne thought. He's either depressed or angry, and I'm not getting anywhere. I'd rather not surprise Brenda and Pat. Maybe the simple gesture of a visit will help clear the air.

* * *

Melba leaned against her office door shaking her head. "You shouldn't have done that," she said.

"Done what?" Suzanne said, smiling, wondering if Melba meant the visit, and if she did, how she found out so quickly.

"Dave told you not to go. I told you it wasn't a good idea."

"Tell me more," Suzanne said. It was her standard response to criticism.

"I suggest you go home before Brenda and Pat get off work." That's all she would say, but Suzanne had no intention of running away in fear.

* * *

Later that afternoon, Loretta arrived in a glittering pink tee shirt and matching jeans, looking far from the typical Presbyterian elder. She's as sweet as Dolly, Suzanne thought, and always has that bright smile like her, too. Together they began to bring the record books up to date. They found six people on the active roll who had died or moved away and fifteen who hadn't been heard from in over a year.

"Thank you, Loretta. I've found this is good to do as soon as I arrive in a church although the records will show that your previous pastor had many more on the rolls when he left than I will. In fact it will look like while I was here, we lost many members."

"Our attendance at worship is back up to sixty, and I think it will keep growing. We'll suggest to the session that these people we've identified need to be taken off the rolls or visited. It's the right thing to do. Speaking of doing the right thing, what's with Brenda and Pat walking out in the middle of Sunday worship?"

"I'd like to talk with them, but they leave before I can."

"That's just tacky," Loretta said. "Downright white trash tacky. Oops, there I go saying what I'm thinking."

"I'm not sure what to do. If I make a big deal out of it, they'll get more attention, which may be what they want. If I ignore it, we're all distracted from our worship. I went over to visit Norm this morning, but he didn't say much, and the women weren't there."

"I'd stay away from there if I were you," Loretta whispered. "You don't want to see them when they get angry."

* * *

That evening as she and Bell had their after dinner coffee, Suzanne described the congregation and the puzzling actions of the former pastor and his family. "Bell, this is a strange situation. I thought I could help the congregation make peace with the past and also see if there is a way for the former pastor to celebrate his ministry there. But now I'm not sure. Do you think maybe I should leave it alone?" Bell pushed back from the table and stretched his long legs. She looked at him over her coffee cup admiring that rugged face she'd loved all these years. The gray that had begun to show in his hair took away nothing. In fact, she thought it added to his distinguished appearance especially when he wore a clergy collar.

"I don't know, Suze. You're much better at that kind of thing than I am," he said. "I've never had a difficult congregation; seems like all of yours are."

"Of course they're difficult. You know I have taken on churches that need help."

"Sure, yeah. Columbus was just right for you and the kids. I guess you're still angry about me taking you away from that."

"No, I like what I'm doing. But it sounded like you were implying that there's something in the way I lead a church that makes for problems."

"Right," he said as he stood up. "I need to get to a meeting." She couldn't tell if she had made her point or if he was being sarcastic.

Maybe I'm being too sensitive, she thought, like Mother always says.

* * *

On Sunday the two women walked out again, but they didn't leave. When Suzanne entered the basement, they stood by the food table talking loudly to Eileen. Suzanne overheard a few words. "You bring too much to eat. Nobody needs all this fattening food." Brenda handed two plates to Pat. "Take these back to the kitchen." Eileen's face screwed up like she was going to cry.

Suzanne moved toward the coffee trying to think if she should intervene and, if so, how. As she turned back to the room sipping from her cup, she saw the two angry women charging toward her. "Stay away from my husband," Brenda said. She pointed at Suzanne and jabbed toward her face. "You don't know how to be a pastor. We can't stand your sermons, Ms. High and Mighty. Stay away from my house."

Pat echoed her mother's words. "Stay away. Reverend Carrollton doesn't need your help."

Suzanne looked Brenda in the eyes and then Pat. "You have nothing to fear from me." She'd learned that phrase from her best friend Frances, a pastor she'd met in Columbus.

Brenda kept jabbing her finger at her and repeating, "You stay away. We don't need you." Pat stood with her arms crossed.

Suzanne swallowed a lump of fear, willing it away, and calmly repeated, "You have nothing to fear from me." Should I ask them to leave, she wondered. The older woman, Brenda, narrowed her eyes and raised her hand like she was going to hit her.

Suzanne stood tall and resisted the temptation to back away.

"You have nothing to fear from me." Brenda narrowed her eyes and stopped her hand in midair.

Dave stood behind Brenda and Pat where they couldn't see him. Eileen joined him. Then Loretta and May. Suzanne felt the presence of others behind her. One by one individuals joined the silent circle of witnesses. They stood there for a holy moment before Brenda saw what was happening. She narrowed her eyes and glared at Suzanne then broke through the circle and stormed out. Pat squinted as though trying to see more clearly and after a moment trailed behind her mother.

Loretta moved from the circle first. She gave Suzanne a hug, and the others began to drift off. She didn't hear anyone talking about what had happened. Suzanne began to tremble.

Loretta put an arm around her shoulders. "Come on, Pastor, let me give you a hand getting things to your car."

The house was empty when she arrived home. There was no one to tell about her morning. She called Frances and described the scene. "Suzanne," she said, "that is really weird. I wonder what you'll discover about those two women. It sounds like a great deal of pain is stored up in them. But, you know, it's quite glorious the way people surrounded you, 'a great cloud of witnesses'."

Chapter 6

Over the next two weeks Dave took Suzanne to visit members who hadn't come to church since she arrived. He introduced her to people in the nursing homes, too. His familiar face and gift of gab made it easy for Suzanne to get acquainted.

He often stopped in at the church to share some news about members of the congregation or offer an idea. One afternoon he sauntered in past the radio blaring country music. (It was Melba's day to pick the station.) He handed Suzanne a cup of coffee from McDonald's and sat across the desk from her. "Pastor," he said, snatching off his Royals cap, "have you ever done a fifth step?"

"Fifth step?"

"Yes, it's part of the twelve step program."

"I only know the first step," she said, "the one about being unable to go on under our own power and the need for a higher power to help us."

"Yes," Dave said, "that's a good summary of one and two."

> *Step one: We admitted we were powerless over alcohol—that our lives had become unmanageable.*
> *Step two: Came to believe that a Power greater than ourselves could restore us to sanity.*
> *Step three: Made a decision to turn our will and our lives over to the care of God as we understood Him.*

> *Step four: Made a searching and fearless moral inventory of ourselves.*
>
> *Step five: Admitted to God, to ourselves, and to another human being the exact nature of our wrongs.*

"You may get requests to do the fifth step. When one of us gets to that point, we need someone we can trust to listen to us. We take it real serious, that searching, fearless moral inventory and admitting exactly what we've done wrong. It's not easy to do a fifth step, and it's not easy to listen to one. Some things people say might shock you."

"I would be honored if someone asked me."

"Good, we need someone trustworthy like you. Maybe you'll go with me to an open meeting, and I can introduce you. A lot of them are members of this church."

"I thought the idea was to be anonymous."

"Some meetings are closed. That's when people share their stuff. But anybody can come to an open meeting. 'Course nobody talks about who's in AA. Norm had a tough time with that. He got to where he would tell things he knew—even in sermons. This past year we tried to work with him. I told him how he'd hurt the recovery of one man, but it didn't seem to sink in. Now, believe me when I say it wasn't like him. Norm wouldn't hurt a fly. But he kept on doing it, and we couldn't go on like that. It wasn't easy. He's helped a lot of us get on the straight and narrow. We finally had to get the Presbytery folks to help us, and Norm didn't take it well."

"Dave, after that disappointment, do you think people will trust another pastor?"

"I think they will trust you."

* * *

Suzanne recognized several members of Lamb of God at her first

AA meeting. Loretta had told her she'd be there and Dave was, of course. She knew Carl, the young man who sat in the first pew on Sundays, looking hungry for something, and Gerald Rains, the nervous man Dave had introduced her to during the fellowship time. His chin still trembled and his eyes darted from person to person. Jim and Marvin, two of the elders, also sat in the circle. That's four out of the six elders, Suzanne thought, counting on her fingers: Loretta, Dave, Jim, and Marvin. The other two are Norm's daughter Pat and sweet eighty-year old May.

The meeting began with introductions: "I'm Jim and I'm an alcoholic." "I'm Loretta and I'm an alcoholic."

Suzanne didn't know what to say. "I'm Suzanne—" She paused. "And I'm glad to meet you."

Dave spoke next, and he helped out, "I brought Suzanne. She's our new pastor, and if you need someone to hear your fifth step, you can trust her."

Loretta wore her spangled jeans and her platinum hair in a big do, as always. She gave a talk about the fourth step. "Don't think you're going to do it quick and easy," she drawled. "You've admitted you can't do this by yourself. You need God. We need God to be our director. He'll provide what we need. So we got to step three, and we said something like this: 'God, I want to do your will. I offer myself to show your love and power.' If we truly stop trying to control life our way and let God show us the way, we find great freedom and hope. Now we're at the fourth step. And we need to do a housecleaning so we can rid ourselves from anything that blocks us from God. I've given you all a blank page to write down your resentments. Follow along with the example on page 65 in *The Big Book*. Write down who you're resentful toward, the cause of the resentment, and how it affects you. Like it says, you have to be fearless. Screw up your courage. Be honest. You've made a commitment to God; now you're trying to find what stands in the way of the new relationship being built up in you.

"We'll pick up here next time. When we have completed the fourth step thoroughly, we'll look at the fifth step, a crucial part of this new life we seek. We will tell a trustworthy person our story. Those of you who have done that, please be ready when we get there to share your experience. I can tell you from experience, doing a fifth step can scare a person out of their wits, so you can help by telling how you did it and survived."

She's something else, Suzanne thought. Not just a pretty face and big hair.

Chapter 7

Suzanne moved through each day on automatic, answering the demands as they came. But her heart wasn't in it. "I have no vision," she told Bell one morning. "I feel stuck. Maybe it's all about the children growing up. They're slipping away from us. How are you handling the thoughts of an empty nest?"

"It's simply another stage of life," he said. "As for your church, pretty soon you'll start planning everyone's life, and it will feel normal."

"What do you mean? That's the opposite of my attitude toward churches I serve." She crossed her arms and hugged herself.

Bell shrugged his shoulders and walked out of the room.

* * *

On Saturday she still felt Bell's comments gnawing at her. He wouldn't talk about it, but she knew who would give her an honest answer: Frances. They had been best friends and confidants since both were pastors in Columbus, Ohio.

The conversation began with the usual catching up, but after a few minutes Frances asked, "How's life?"

"It's rather dull," Suzanne said. "I can't seem to get enthusiastic about this church. Not sure why."

"What else is going on?"

"Peter will be leaving for college in ten weeks. It seems like the most unnatural thing in the world, yet I know it isn't."

"What else?" Frances asked.

Suzanne hesitated. "I want to ask you something because I know I can count on you to give me a straight, honest answer. Bell said pretty soon I'd be planning everyone's life at church. Do you think I do that?"

Frances hesitated. "Let me think about this. You're organized, and you like everything around you to be organized. That's mostly a good trait, one I've always admired. It seems to me that you've loosened up on that lately when the churches in Kansas needed something different from strategic planning. But in general, I think if you ever carried to excess your natural inclination to have things orderly, it could be controlling. Nevertheless, I've never experienced you trying to plan everybody's life. Have you asked him to tell you more?"

"Yes, he turns and walks away. He seems angry all the time lately. I'm worried about his drinking. Maybe I've nagged him too much about that. Frances, I don't remember ever being this sad before in my whole life."

"Are you depressed?"

"I don't know."

"Are you sleeping all right?"

"Yes," Suzanne said, "no change."

"Are you more tired than usual?"

"A little."

"Are you eating more or less than usual?"

"Less, a lot less."

"Do you put on a happy face to hide feelings of sadness?"

"Yes. I have to do that at church."

"Have you lost interest in things you used to enjoy?"

"I can't remember enjoying anything. But I must have had fun helping the girls get ready for the prom. I can't remember."

"Suzanne, you might be depressed, or it might be a temporary time of sadness. Have you and Bell made any plans for your empty nest time, like taking a trip or some other way of enjoying your new freedom together?"

"We haven't talked about it much. He doesn't seem to be feeling sad at all. He says it's a normal next stage of life. I'll keep aware of depression symptoms. Surely I'll snap out of this soon."

* * *

After summer vacation began, Julie and Peter spent nearly every day with Sarah and Matthew Edwards. Suzanne couldn't help thinking what good life partners they'd make. She and Jewell had sworn each other to secrecy after confessing their hopes. But they weren't the only ones who thought the two couples belonged together. Once, Matthew and Sarah's older brother Robert had whispered to Suzanne, "Wouldn't it be awesome if Peter and Sarah ended up a couple like Matthew and Julie?"

Peter and Julie asked Suzanne and Bell to meet with them and the Edwards family to talk about summer job plans, but it was hard to find a date when Bell would be at home. Peter was more insistent and bossy than Suzanne had ever seen him. He cornered his dad with dates everyone else could get together, and it was settled. Sarah, Matthew, and their parents would come to Salina for pizza and to hear the plans.

At seven o'clock on the designated Friday evening, not only Matthew, Sarah and their parents walked in, but also their brother Robert. Laughter surrounded them as always. Ed had a new joke. "I heard on the radio today that each of us eats over a ton of dirt a day."

"Oh, come on, that can't be true," Julie said. "What's the punchline?"

"No, it's true," Ed said. "Ask Jewell. Isn't it true, sweetheart?"

She nodded and everyone else waited. But Ed left it at that and went on talking to Bell about fishing until Sarah couldn't stand it anymore.

"Dad, how can that be true about eating dirt?"

Ed put on his innocent looking face and wiggled his eyebrows at his daughter. "You probably eat over not one but two tons of dirt a day if you consider how far it is to China."

Matthew and Peter groaned in unison. "Eating over dirt," Peter said.

They sat down around the dining room table, and Julie took the lead. "We've been thinking about how to earn money this summer, and we want your opinions. Remember that year we took care of children in the summers in Middletown? We'd like to do that again."

Matthew said, "Do you think we could do that here in Salina some days and some days in Middletown? There isn't much for kids to do in the summer unless their parents send them to camp for a week. We'd have the parents drop them off at a park, and we'd show them a good time, maybe teach them some games or sports. Then their parents could pick them up at a set time."

I usually speak up quickly at times like this, Suzanne thought. Maybe that's why Bell thinks I am controlling. I still don't think I am, but let's see what happens if I hold back.

They had already put together a good plan, having considered security, safety, legal permission from parents, and what they would charge. Suzanne wondered why they had asked all of them to be there. The kids already had it figured out, and all four parents agreed that it looked like a good, solid plan. "Go for it," Ed said. "You boys are going to need spending money at college, and you girls always seem to need more shoes." The girls rolled their eyes in unison.

Jewell disappeared and came back carrying a cake covered with candles and singing "Happy Birthday" to Suzanne. "You didn't think we forgot your birthday, did you?" she said.

"But it was weeks ago," Suzanne said.

"I declare this to be your birthday," Ed said. "And that's not all."

Robert handed her a box. A little furry head poked out knocking the top to the floor. "This is Wolfie and he needs a home."

"He's a long-haired Chihuahua," Sarah said.

The fluffy ball looked up at Suzanne with huge, golden-brown eyes, and she lifted him onto her lap. "He's adorable," she said. "Look at you, you are so soft. Oh, I love him." She hugged him to her. "Thank you."

"We know you're at work all day, but lots of executives are taking their dogs to work with them." Robert said. "It's the latest thing. We brought a little crate for him to sleep in, and he likes it. To him it's like a cave. And here's the big gift: Mother trained him. He's housebroken."

Jewell grinned. "Suzanne, I told them it's not good to give a pet as a surprise gift. And if it's not a good time for you, I'll be glad to keep him."

"Ha, you stop thinking you'll keep this dog. He's already attached to me. See, he's all cuddly and comfortable right here on my lap. But I tell you what, you can visit any time."

By now Bell was sitting in his recliner. As usual one cat draped itself around the back of his chair, and the other two sat in his lap. She took the dog over to meet him. "Look, Bell. This is Wolfie."

The cats scattered. Bell petted him. "Cute," he said, looking around her to see the TV. "Homerun," he yelled.

"Mom, are you crying?" Julie asked.

"You all don't know how much I love this little pup already." Wolfie turned in her arms, looked her in the eyes, and reached a paw up to her tears. She buried her face in his fur. "Did I thank you?"

* * *

Wolfie became her constant companion. At the office he sat on a blanket beside her desk or in his crate. Melba came in to give him a treat every morning. Suzanne was pleased to see how she mellowed around the little pup. So far no one who visited the office had an allergy to dogs, so he became a fixture at the church. Some people stopped by simply to see him. It's a good excuse to come in, Suzanne thought, easier than making a formal appointment. Already one woman had brought him a blanket and stayed to talk about difficulties she was having with her daughter.

Every day after lunch she took Wolfie for a walk. This will be a good way to get acquainted with the people around the church, Suzanne thought. She went a different direction every afternoon. First she walked west, away from the main road. Here pavement gave way quickly to gravel and then dirt paths. A trailer home sat here, a disheveled house there. In one yard a circle of webbed chairs and benches sat under an old cottonwood tree, one of few large trees she'd seen on the streets around the church.

She heard footsteps behind her and tensed. I don't know anything about this neighborhood and probably shouldn't be here by myself. Wolfie isn't much of a guard dog.

She turned around to see the young man who sat in the first pew every Sunday. He always looked vulnerable and open; "hungry" had been her thought on the first day. "Carl, hello. Do you live around here?"

He took off his cap and ran his hand through his hair. "Yes, Pastor. That's where I live, the house across the road there." He pointed to a green cottage which looked like it couldn't be more than one room. "Dave owns it. He's letting me stay there until I get my feet back under me. I'm trying to work the program again. I got on at Boeing, and I can't mess up this time. I wonder, could you … would you hear my fifth step some time?"

"Of course I will. I'd be honored to do that with you. When?"

He pulled pieces of paper out of his pocket. "I'm ready, I think."

"We're headed back to the church. Shall we go ahead then or do you want to wait until tomorrow?"

"I'd like to do it today ... if you can."

They sat in the sanctuary, him in the front pew, Suzanne on a choir chair facing him. Wolfie sat quietly on her lap. "As I understand it," she said, "we want uninterrupted time, and this is confidential. From the talk I heard at an open meeting, this is to be a positive time although some unpleasant truths may be spoken. We come together in the presence of God, seeking to be cleansed. And from what I hear, you can expect to feel better afterward. Do I have this right?"

"Yep, yep, that's it."

"Okay, Carl. You go at whatever pace you want to. We have all the time in the world. I told Melba not to interrupt us."

He took a deep breath. "I need to start way back when I was six years old." He teared up and paused a long time. "I seen my father rape my older sister. I shoulda done something about it, and I always felt guilty that I didn't. And, and angry." His face turned red and his hands made fists. "I know in my mind that I couldn't have stopped him. And my anger isn't doing any good. Still those thoughts are in me." He hit his chest with his fist. "So deep in me. I want to get them out, but I don't know how. I made the fearless inventory, and this is the next step, but I don't know. I get all tangled up. It's the first time I've gotten this far."

"Yes, I can see this is difficult," Suzanne said and waited to see if he would go on.

After a long pause, she asked, "Do you have children?"

He hung his head lower, then cut his eyes up. "I have a little girl Ella. She's eleven now. I worry about her." There was a long pause. Suzanne prayed silently, *God, help this man. He's in deep pain. Please give him courage for this moment.*

"I have nightmares, especially after my sister told me our

grandfather said a girl's duty was to please the men around her, but he wasn't sure she had what it took. She did everything to please him, and he took advantage of that. Both my dad and his dad. I should've done something."

This is supposed to be a positive experience, Suzanne thought. But he's mired down with negativity. "What's different now?" she asked.

"I don't think like they did about women," he said vehemently sitting up straighter. "And I could stop such a thing now that I'm older."

"And would you?"

"Oh, yes. AA has helped me a lot. And I think it's true that I can't handle this by myself. I've tried that. I know that I have to depend on God."

"Is there something else from your fearless inventory you haven't resolved?"

"Yes."

His tears started, and he couldn't wipe them away fast enough. Finally he gave up trying. Suzanne wished she had brought tissues. She stayed very still, but Wolfie woke up. He jumped from her lap to Carl's and pawed at his face.

Laughing through the tears, Carl hugged the pup to him. "I know it's probably not logical, but I wonder if I will be like my dad and my granddad as Ella … you know, grows up."

"Do thoughts like that tempt you to drink again?"

"Yes."

"What do you tell yourself when that happens?"

He answered quickly. "One step at a time. Rely on God. Work the program. Walk the walk."

"God is with you, Carl. It's clear to me you are a courageous and strong man who wants to do what's best for his daughter even if it means staying away from her."

"But I want to be part of her life."

"What will it take for that to happen?"

"Staying with AA. And I need to make amends to those I've hurt."

"Who is that?"

"My sister. But I've already done that. We've had long talks. She asks me what I could have done to protect her. We couldn't come up with anything. And I've told her I'm sorry I didn't even try. I didn't understand exactly what was going on, but I knew she was being hurt."

"Anyone else?"

"I don't know what to say to Stacey—that's my wife—and Ella, but I owe them something .... We're not supposed to confess something just to get it off our shoulders if it will hurt someone else, so I don't know ...."

"What has hurt them?"

"I guess the drinking and not being with them." He looked up. "Yes, I need to ask them to forgive me for that. And I need to be strong so we can live together again, and I can be a good husband and dad. I know I would never hurt either of them—as long as I'm not drinking."

His forehead smoothed out and his eyes lightened. "Thank you, thank you." He kissed Wolfie on the top of his little head.

"I believe you can do this, Carl. Is there anything else on your inventory that you need to say out loud?"

"No, no, I feel so ... um, my shoulders feel lighter. That's what's supposed to happen, isn't it?"

"That's what I hear." Suzanne smiled. "Do you want to pray?"

He nodded. "Will you start?"

She wanted to hold his hands, but he held Wolfie in his lap, so she put her hands on the dog's head.

> *God our creator and defender. You who have given birth to us and walked with us every day of our lives, we give you thanks for leading Carl to this moment. He has worked hard to understand*

what makes him want to drink and what can deliver him from that demon. But he has acknowledged that it's beyond his control to do that without you.

Carl took over.

Thank you, thank you. Stay with me, please. I need you close by every day. Protect Ella and Stacey. And me. Thank you for my AA group. Thank you for my church. Help me find the right words to say to Ella and Stacey. Amen.

Chapter 8

IGNORING Melba's advice about where to walk the dog, Suzanne headed south one day. Norm stood in his weedy but green yard behind a push mower. He leaned on it and hung his head. Should I stop and speak, Suzanne wondered. He may be avoiding eye contact. Then he began to slip sideways. She reached him in time and held him up until she felt his legs stiffen, then half carried him with one arm and pulled Wolfie's leash with the other.

Once inside she sat him down in a kitchen chair and wet a dish towel to wipe his face. He breathed hard, and she considered calling an ambulance. But in a few moments he asked for water and looked as if he had recovered.

The smell of cats and rotting food nearly overcame her, and she left him for a moment to take out the garbage and the cat box. She was outside the kitchen door when Pat drove up. Hurrying inside, Suzanne hoped she could get Wolfie and leave by the front door quickly to avoid Pat. The car door slammed. Suzanne, forgetting all else, stopped in the doorway and stared at Norm. He had taken his shirt off and held Wolfie, trying to get his leash undone. Black and blue bruises covered the man's back. Suzanne gently touched his shoulder, and he cringed folding into himself and cradling the soft fur to his chest.

Then the back door slammed and Pat charged at her. "What have you done to my dad?" She grabbed the dog and thrust him at Suzanne. "You better hope Mom doesn't get here before you leave."

Norm reached out to take Wolfie back. "Call Buddy. Get Buddy."

"My brother Billy," Pat whispered. "He died in Viet Nam."

"Pat, your dad fainted while mowing the grass. We were walking by and helped him into the house."

"Why is his shirt off?"

"Why are there bruises?" Suzanne asked.

Pat started to speak then stopped. Finally, she said, "He falls a lot."

"Pat, someone has been hitting this man. Is it you?"

"No," she looked frightened. "No, I would never do that."

"Your mother?"

She looked away.

"Pat, what are you going to do about this?"

"What do you want me to do? Call the cops?"

"Pat ...."

Norm stared at the two of them. "Help me," he whimpered.

"Either you take him to the emergency room or I will," Suzanne said.

"I'll take him."

Suzanne helped her get him into the car. "You call me by two o'clock and let me know how he is, or I will call the authorities."

"Okay," Pat said. She angrily swiped at a tear. "It's his own fault. If only he'd listen to Mom."

"There is no excuse for this," Suzanne said.

* * *

"You should have called the police," Bell said. "What were you thinking?"

"I thought he should get help immediately and the hospital would call social services. Pat did call me from the ER and said they were admitting him."

"How do you get into these predicaments?" Bell asked. "Sounds to me like you're messing with dangerous people."

"What would you have done?"

"The minute I saw those bruises I'd have called the police."

"Maybe I should have," she said. "Bell, they probably sound like a rough bunch of people, but many of them came to the church as a result of their AA experience with the twelve steps. I'm impressed with what they're learning about confession and forgiveness," she said. "It's all in confidence, of course, but I can say that one man had some heavy guilt on his back. In the fourth step he made a fearless inventory of his life and anyone he hurt. Then in the fifth step he confessed it aloud to another person—me, to God, and to himself. He'd done some hard work, and the confession led him to a freedom so strong I could almost see it. It was beautiful."

"We do that every Sunday," Bell said. "Don't you have a prayer of confession and assurance of pardon?"

"Yes, of course. But this is different. Down the road he will make amends where he can. It's the reality of what we talk about in church but rarely see heartfelt evidence of."

She busied herself in the kitchen chopping potatoes and carrots to go into stew for dinner. She felt some of her frustration lessen. She slid a loaf of bread into the oven. She had mixed it in the morning and left it in the refrigerator to rise. But later when the oven timer went off, she found the loaf had slumped in the middle. It was hard and inedible. What did I mess up, she wondered? Did I add the salt twice? I can't seem to do anything right.

* * *

The next day the nurse in ICU gave Suzanne an update. "He has a broken rib, multiple contusions, and bruises all over him. We'll set a break in his wrist this afternoon. Malnutrition is a major complication, which we're addressing; and as we gain ground there, his mental state may improve. He keeps asking for Buddy. Do you know who that is?"

"His son who died in Viet Nam. He seems to think he's still alive."

"I see. Go on in. Maybe you can comfort him."

"Has his wife Brenda been here?"

"No, only his daughter who cries all the time. But she hasn't been back since the police came and questioned her. Somebody has been beating this poor man."

The minute she drew the curtain back on his cubicle, he opened his eyes. "Hi," he said. "Where's Wolfie?" Norm's eyes looked clearer and more focused. Any time she'd seen him before, his eyes wandered and had a dazed look about them.

"Sorry, Norm. I couldn't bring him in here. How are you feeling?"

"I'm better. They have good food and television." He pointed to cartoon characters dancing. "Pat brought me here, but she didn't come back. And Brenda hasn't come yet. I'm worried about them."

"I'll call Melba and ask her to check on them," Suzanne said.

Later Dave walked in, and Suzanne offered a prayer before leaving him and Norm to talk.

> *God Almighty, you give us comfort when we need it. You bring us friends and companions and doctors and nurses to help us. We ask you to work through the people who serve you here and all those who care about Norm. You bring the healing of your Holy Spirit. We ask you to let that spirit blow like a mighty wind to heal Norm's body and his spirit. We pray in Jesus' name. Amen.*

"Will you wait for me?" Dave asked. "I need to talk to you about something."

Suzanne called the church office and asked Melba to see if Brenda and Pat were home. "I want to let them know Norm is asking for them."

Then she sat down near the hospital entry to wait for Dave. She had closed her eyes for a moment when a soft voice said, "Pastor Suzanne?"

She looked up to see Loretta. "How's Norm?"

"He's better. Dave's with him. I don't know where Pat and Brenda are. Melba's trying to find them."

"That's strange. Did Dave tell you about his daughter?"

"Daughter? I thought he and Eileen had two sons."

She shook her head. "Dave will tell you. I'll be back soon." She sounded different, softer. A sweet southern drawl replaced the country twang. And instead of the sparkle and denim she wore all the time—even to church—she had on a green blouse with a high lace neck under a white suit.

* * *

About thirty minutes later Dave and Loretta returned. Dave looked down at the floor. "It's sad to see Norm like this."

"Sure is," Loretta said. "We owe him a lot. He helped Dave and me both when we were down and out. Got us on the twelve steps."

"He helped me get back on track more than once," Dave said. "He's going to need our help now." He sighed. "But the reason I asked you to wait for me is I wonder if you'd help me find my daughter? I think she's living somewhere down here in the middle of the city."

"How can I help?"

"She's been in several recovery programs, and I'm thinking we could check around, see if we can find out where she is now. Some places people will talk to me, but Lizzie's more likely to talk to Loretta. Then I'm thinking people who run rehab centers might talk to a pastor."

"Sure, I'll help," Suzanne said.

"First, we'll treat you to the best cheeseburgers in the world," Loretta said. "We used to go there in the old days."

* * *

"Hey, it's our Dolly," the bartender called out to the mid-day crowd. "Look at you! All dressed up. Where you dancing these days?"

"Lordy, Jim, I haven't been dancing for years. You know that." The twang was back.

"We can always hope," he said and winked. "I hear you on the radio every now and again. That first record you made was the best."

"I'm singing good ol' gospel songs nowadays," she said. "If you come to the Winfield festival, look me up. Get you some religion."

"Three cheeseburgers, Jim," Dave said. "How about you girls find a booth, and I'll join you in a minute." They left Dave talking to Jim at the bar while they found seats.

"What's that about Winfield?" Suzanne asked as they took a seat. "My son starts college there this fall."

"Honey, that's a real nice Methodist school they got there and Winfield has the best bluegrass festival ever. It's the International Flat-picking Championships. You put it on your calendar, third weekend in September. Now I see that doubt on your face, but bluegrass is lots of kinds of music. There's cowboy songs and folk music and you'll even hear some classical over at the mandolin contest. You ever hear of John McCutcheon, the folk singer? You'd like him. Trust me. If you like music, you'll like this festival."

"I like music festivals," Suzanne said. And, she thought, that will give me a chance to see Peter a few weeks after school starts. "I've been meaning to ask about the records you've made."

"I just love to sing. And I've done okay with it. But when I got sober, I left behind dancing and singing in places like this. Like the song says, 'Thanks to Calvary, we don't come here anymore.'"

Dave brought cheeseburgers and Cokes to the table. "I hope you like this, Suzanne, since we've bragged on them. Now, I need to tell you that Eileen doesn't know I'm doing this. She disowned Liz 'cause she stole her mother's ring and her grandmother's brooch to buy drugs. We've been disappointed over and over again. But I can't stop myself from hoping."

"It's been hard on Eileen," Loretta said. "And Brenda made it worse. She's been real hurtful saying it's her and Dave's fault their daughter is addicted."

"Well, my alcoholism hasn't helped," Dave said. "Brenda's quick to point that out. Anyway, Lizzy's been through treatment three times—that I know of," Dave said. "She used to come here a lot especially when Loretta was singing. We thought someone might have seen her."

"We became good friends," Loretta said. "Later, she came to AA and was doing real well. She asked me to be her sponsor. But then she started going with that dirt bag Joey, who gave her drugs." She banged her fist on the table. "No matter what, I'm not giving up on that girl. Mama and Grand Mama never gave up on me. They moved here all the way from Alabama to help me survive when I went through detox. I'm going to be like that for Liz."

Dave nodded toward Jim who was making the rounds of the tables. "Jim heard she went to Mother Mary's, a treatment center. It's not far from here. He's asking some folks if they've seen her lately. These treatment centers can be real secretive. That's why I asked you to come, Suzanne. They may talk to a pastor."

When Jim reached them, he said, "I don't know if it's true, but one of the guys said he heard she had a baby. That would fit with Mother Mary's. They'd help her there."

Dave stared at the man and kept staring as he walked away. "A baby," he murmured.

Loretta grinned. "That would make you a granddad, Dave. Just think, a little girl or a little boy that looks like you."

Dave grinned back, then his eyes widened. "We have to find that child. No telling what conditions she's growing up in."

"Or he," Loretta said. "Yes, we have to find Liz. I wonder what Eileen will say about being a grandmother … if this is true, that is."

Dave sucked in his breath. "Maybe that will turn Eileen around."

Before they left, Suzanne called Melba to see if she'd talked to Brenda and Pat. "No, no answer at the house. I went over there and nobody's home. The car's gone. I'll try again before I go home. Maybe they are at the hospital."

Suzanne reported back to Dave and Loretta. "Melba says she hasn't seen Brenda or Pat, and nobody answers the phone or the door. I called the hospital. The nurse says they haven't been there. I'm uneasy about them, but I'm not sure what else I can do even if I rush back. Let's go on and see what we can find out about your daughter."

* * *

At Mother Mary's they decided Suzanne would go in alone first and ask whether they might visit Liz—if she was there—or get any information about her.

Sister Johanna talked with Suzanne a long time, explaining their services, their needs for financial assistance, and their policies. But she wouldn't tell her if Liz had ever been there. "We work with strict rules of confidentiality. I'm sure you understand."

"Yes, I do," Suzanne said. "I came in alone in case there would be an exception for her pastor. Her father and her AA sponsor are waiting in the car."

In the hallway, a young man bounced a basketball and yelled, "We'll get you next time. This was just practice. We'll catch you next week."

Sister Johanna opened her door. "Billy, come, meet Pastor Suzanne. She's here looking for information about Liz Perkins. I told her we keep strict confidentiality."

Suzanne shook hands with him. "We'd like to get word to Liz that her father wants to speak with her. If either of you see her, would you give her that message?"

"Yes, if … if she ever comes in here, I will give her that message," Sister Johanna said. "And Billy, you do the same." They exchanged phone numbers, and the woman gave her a sympathetic smile and a warm handshake before they walked her out. Suzanne had to go back to Dave and Loretta with little information and the news that neither of them would get anywhere with Sister Johanna either.

They were pulling away from the curb when Suzanne looked at the contact information. "Stop. Stop, Dave." She jumped out of the car and ran back down the sidewalk. "Billy," she yelled.

She caught up with them as they opened the door to go in. "Billy, I see your last name is Carrollton. Are you related to Norm Carrollton?"

He hesitated. "I used to be."

"You look like him. Did he call you, 'Buddy'?"

"Yes."

"We came here from the hospital. He's at Wesley Medical Center and keeps calling for Buddy. Pat told me you died in Vietnam."

"I sorta did." He glanced at Sister Johanna. "I came back real messed up."

"This is quite a coincidence, meeting you today."

He grinned and Sister Johanna chuckled. "We have a saying here, 'There are no coincidences,'" she said.

By now Loretta and Dave had joined them, and after Suzanne explained and introduced everyone, Dave said, "What a coincidence."

***

Later, over dinner, Suzanne told Bell, Julie and Peter about her day. "Finding Norm's son Billy was the most amazing thing. Then Dave took me back to the hospital to get my car, and Billy went with us. He wasn't going to until we told him his mother and sister hadn't been at home or back to the hospital since Norm was admitted. It's an answer to prayer. If Brenda and Pat have left town—and they may have since the police are looking for them—Norm will be all alone without anyone to care for him."

"Why are the police looking for them?" Peter asked.

"Somebody's been beating him up," Bell answered.

Julie turned to her dad. "That's awesome about finding Norm's son. What do you think about coincidences like that?"

"I guess the answer is found in the law of probability" Bell said. "Sometimes things like that are going to happen, but it's superstitious to believe God caused your mom to meet Norm's son."

"Mom?"

"Hmmm. Superstitious? I think of superstition as believing you can do a certain thing to get God to do what you want. In this kind of situation I'm torn between believing it's one of those accidental happenings in life or that it's one way God is still creating."

"Like that weaving thing?" Julie asked.

"Yes, God is so creative that whatever happens in life, all things are woven together in a beautiful whole cloth."

"That's kinda like when we say we can't control what happens to us but we can control how we respond," Peter said.

"I think that's different," Julie said, "but true."

"If we all do the best we can to live according to God's laws, we help good things happen," Bell said. "That's what I believe. Do what you can to help other people, then it's up to them. Move on. Someone else will come and you will help them." He yawned and stood up. "Too much theology for me," he said. "I'm off duty."

* * *

"Peter, have you made a list of what you need to take to college?" Suzanne yelled up the stairs one morning.

"It's in my head, Mom. I don't need to write it down."

"You'll be surprised how many little things you'll need for dorm life."

"Okay, okay. Stop worrying about everything. I'll think about it later."

Suzanne was torn. She wanted to make a list for him, but he'd made it clear he was taking care of getting himself ready. However, items kept coming to her mind, and finally she wrote them down. I'll make this list, so I won't keep thinking about it. Then later I'll decide whether to offer it to him. We'll have to go shopping. He probably hasn't thought of that. She wrote down a quick list and shoved it into the junk drawer as she heard two sets of feet running down the stairs.

Peter ran into the kitchen and kissed her on the cheek. "Off to the park and the kiddos. This is a really good summer job," he said.

Julie was right behind him. "Sure is. Those kids are having lots of fun," she said. "No time for breakfast. We'll grab something at McDonald's."

Suzanne pulled her calendar out of her purse. How many days until he leaves, she wondered. She sat at the kitchen table and counted, one by one, how many days she had left with her family together.

I will treasure each day, she thought. How many times in the past did I do something else instead of enjoying him? Her heart hurt. Pictures flashed through her mind: newborn Peter with big blue eyes and hair that stuck straight up, the toddler sitting with her on a blanket in the yard, him bravely walking in the kindergarten door. I'm glad I stayed home with him and Julie these past three years after that terrifying summer when the tree limb fell on him.

God, forgive me if I made wrong choices. I believe you called me to be a pastor, and you called me to be a mother and a wife. Have I heard you right? She waited, but the silence was infinite. She tried again. God, am I asking the wrong questions? Do you have a plan for my life? If you do, it would be so much easier if I knew what it was. Or should I simply take each day and make the best of it? I don't even know what that means. Please let me hear you speaking clearly.

I should be writing in my journal, she thought. When did I stop doing that?

Chapter 9

Loretta visited Norm every other day and reported that he was better and much calmer with Billy around. No one had heard from Brenda and Pat, but a neighbor told Dave she had seen them putting suitcases in their car and driving off.

When Suzanne went to the hospital the next Monday, Norm wasn't there. He had been moved to a rehab facility. She found the building across from the hospital and sat with Billy at the edge of an exercise room watching Norm practice walking up and down stairs.

Billy slumped over and rubbed his eyes. "Dad keeps asking me to find Mother and Pat. I don't know what to say. Surely he realizes that Mother hit him repeatedly and Pat allowed it to go on." He looked at Suzanne. "The police are looking for them, but they have little to go on except Mother's car was sold last week in Laredo."

Suzanne searched for what to say, but nothing came to her. She nodded, and he went on. "It's crazy. I wonder what happened to her. Mother was always so proper. She said we had a responsibility as the pastor's family. She drilled us on the Bible. And she always kept us looking good. If we didn't have money for new clothes, she'd make them. She thrived on being a pastor's daughter and the pastor's wife."

"What was she like when you came back from Vietnam?"

Suzanne asked as they watched Norm move to another exercise area where he put groceries from a counter top onto a shelf.

Billy was quiet. Finally he said, "I was so messed up I didn't know where I was half the time. PTSD they said. Even firecrackers on the fourth of July set me off, and there was no telling what I would do. I was wild. I think Dad left the church he was in at the time 'cause Mother was embarrassed by me. She told me not to come 'round the new church, but I didn't know she told people I was dead—until you told me. Lately, I'd been thinking about trying to see them, now that I'm sober and relatively normal. But I've been taking life one day at a time and wasn't quite ready to be with them. Now, I'm thinking I'll move in and take care of Dad if they don't come back."

"Did you know your dad had begun acting erratically, saying things from the pulpit that were confidential? Maybe it was hard on your mother when he had to give up being a minister and she had to give up being the minister's wife."

"Yes, it would be. It sure would be. No more status, no image to uphold. All the things that had meaning for her. I can sorta see that. But I can't come to grips with Mother or Pat hurting Dad."

* * *

Suzanne asked Peter and Julie to provide music at Lamb of God church one Sunday. "I'd like for the people to meet you and you to meet them. After church we could go to a good barbecue place I found."

"Maybe," Peter said clearing the table after supper.

"When could you let me know?" Suzanne asked.

"Aw, Mom," Julie said sitting with her chin in her palm. "We've been working hard. It's not easy keeping up with little kids every day. Right now I'm too tired, but I might feel like it by Sunday morning."

"Hmmm," Suzanne said getting up from the table. "Okay,

I hope you can. The sermon is the parable of the workers in the vineyard. The one Jesus tells about the laborers who worked only a short time getting as much pay as those who worked a long time."

"Julie," Peter yelled from the kitchen, "don't we have a song that goes with that? Something we sang at Middletown a long time ago? Work and grace were in the words."

"I don't remember," she said.

Peter poked his head back into the dining room. "Why are you so grouchy?"

"I'm not grouchy. I'm just tired. Leave me alone."

"You are too grouchy. Ever since Matthew talked to that hot girl at the park this morning you've been moping around. Snap out of it! You have him wrapped around your little finger. You two should go ahead and get married so you don't have to worry about that kind of thing."

Julie made a face at him and stomped up the stairs to her room.

* * *

They did sing, and they met the people. Loretta intrigued them, and they sang with her after church in fellowship hall. Everyone joined in on "I'll Fly Away."

"You always find the best churches," Julie said on the way home.

* * *

Suzanne had never known a congregation to be so attentive in worship. They seemed to need it; they seemed to enjoy it, especially the singing. The hymns they sang weren't the ones Suzanne would have chosen. The theology in them was often questionable, and there was more reference to dying than to living, but they sang with gusto and the music lifted everyone up into joy.

Loretta chose the hymns. She was good at considering the scriptures for the day and then choosing from the songs most people knew. She refused to use any that dragged. "What good is a song if you don't go home singing it?" she asked Suzanne.

Suzanne began to suspect that some individuals came to the church as a result of attending one of the AA groups that met there and probably through Dave's invitation. He and Loretta often brought visitors. Some of them, like Carl, became regulars. Several weeks after his fifth step with Suzanne, he brought his wife Stacey and their eleven-year-old daughter Ella.

Not all the worshippers came from AA though. Suzanne met many of the longtime members through May, who had been there since childhood. May and her friends often brought their grandchildren.

And so they began a one-room Sunday school for children of all ages. May taught it, and when Julie was there, she helped. "I love those little children," May said. "They are so fresh and open; they see the world with new eyes. I like the curriculum you gave me. It introduces them to God's world and God's people, and it tells Bible stories they can understand."

Suzanne encouraged her to continue forming relationships with the children, and they made plans to incorporate them into the worshipping congregation. They began having a time for children in the worship service. Wolfie sat with them, and they each gave him hugs before they went back to their seats.

Suzanne began a sermon series on the parables of Jesus, searching out the core meaning in each one and then telling a story which showed it coming alive in the current day. As she wrote those sermons, she often thought of the people working through the twelve steps. Even those who weren't could benefit from them—including herself. She kept a copy of the steps on her desk and often consulted the eleventh one when writing sermons.

Sought through prayer and meditation to improve our conscious contact with God, as we understood Him, praying only for knowledge of His will for us and the power to carry that out.

Often at the fellowship time after church Suzanne found herself at a table with someone who had a question about the sermon that day. When their questions taxed her memory, she'd go to her office for a reference book. May began to be interested in that treasure trove of information. When Peter was there, he delighted May by being as curious as she was. They'd put their heads together over Bible dictionaries and commentaries to find answers. Others who had questions began asking them to find out what they wanted to know. These people are different, Suzanne thought. They're hungrier than most parishioners I've known.

CHAPTER 10

Suzanne sat beside some newly found clergy friends at a Presbytery meeting in the sanctuary of Grace Presbyterian Church in Wichita. They listened to an introduction of the new Executive Presbyter, Paige Rex. Although Suzanne was a member of the Presbytery of Northern Kansas, as an interim in the territory of the Presbytery of Southern Kansas, she also attended their meetings. Report after report droned on. Suzanne was restless. She was used to doing more than one thing at a time and wanted to check her calendar. However, she felt constrained by the formality of the moment and her newness to that group.

An usher walked down the aisle showing a paper to several people. One finally pointed in her direction and people in her pew passed a message over to her.

"Call me immediately," it said and had her home phone number. Her heart stopped for a moment. Peter? Julie? Bell?

She gathered her papers, stepped over her colleagues' feet, and found her way to the office. It took her three times to enter her phone credit card number correctly and make the connection.

Bell answered. "Bell, what's wrong?"

"I need you to come home immediately," he said.

"Bell, tell me. What is it? Peter? Julie?"

"No, they're fine."

"Are you sick? What's wrong?"

"Nobody's sick. But I need you to come home right now. It's important."

"Okay. I'm leaving now. I'll be there in, I don't know, an hour and a half, maybe a little more. Can't you give me some idea of what's wrong so I don't worry all the way?"

"Everything."

"Tell me what's wrong."

"It's everything. I need you to come home right now."

"I'm on my way. Hang on."

Suzanne sped up to pull in front of a long line of trucks on I 135. I wonder why there is so much traffic on a Saturday afternoon. It's going to take me much longer to get home. She glanced at her mobile phone on the seat next to her. Still not in range, not even a roaming signal. When I'm closer, I'll call him. No, that will make him angry. I'll wait. What could possibly be wrong? He said "Everything," but the children aren't sick. Did he say he wasn't sick? "Everything," what could that mean? It has to be about his church. When his work gets tough, he always thinks the sky is falling. I hope he hasn't made up his mind to leave First Presbyterian. Then again, he hasn't mentioned any trouble. Surely it's not the church. But if it is and he takes another church, it will have to be in Kansas. The kids will be in Kansas. I can't bear to leave them here and move away. Besides, if we move it's my turn to accept a call and him to follow. But we need to consider the salary offered, especially with five more years of the kids in college. He'll always be offered a better salary than I will. What else could it be? My parents, my sisters? No, he said "Everything."

Newton, Hesston, McPherson, Lindsborg, Gypsum. The signs marched by and then the billboards for Salina and its exits began to show: Shilling, Magnolia, and finally Crawford.

She slowed down to take the ramp. Her stomach hurt, her heart beat uneasily, and her breath stopped in her throat. This had better be important after calling me out of a Presbytery meeting and scaring me out of my wits.

Finally, she pulled into the garage. She found Bell at the kitchen table, two beer bottles in front of him. His shoulders slumped, he hadn't shaved. He wore an old stretched out sweatshirt.

"So what's wrong?" Suzanne asked. "You look like hell."

"Everything."

"Everything?"

She waited, knowing from experience that begging him to talk would get her nowhere. She sat down. She stared at him. He stared at the table.

Finally, he said, "My whole life is about to change."

She waited. He continued staring at the table. "Bell, tell me. You know we can handle anything."

"I'm leaving the church," he said.

"Have you received a call from another one?"

"No."

"Bell, please tell me what's happened," she said controlling her voice. She took a deep breath and let it out slowly, trying to prepare herself.

He shook his head. "I don't want to do this anymore. I'm leaving."

"Leaving?"

"Starting over. We've raised the kids. They're going to be okay. You're working again. You'll be fine."

"You're not making any sense. Talk to me. What's going on with you?"

He took a drink from the bottle but didn't say anything.

"What do you plan to do?" she asked.

"That won't concern you anymore," he said.

"Of course it will. Anything that affects you affects me—and Peter and Julie, too. Bell, tell me why you called me to come home. What's the emergency?"

"Didn't you hear me?" He pushed his chair back scraping the floor and stood up, towering over her. His face squinched into an angry mask. His voice came out harsh and guttural. No tears. All anger. "I'm leaving. I'm starting over, a new life. We can make our own agreement."

"What?"

"We've always worked well together. I think we can handle this on our own."

"Handle what?"

"What do you think I've been telling you?"

"I don't know. You haven't told me what's wrong yet. Did something happen at the church?"

"Listen to me," he screeched. "I'm ... leaving ... everything. New. Life. Don't be so dense. You think this is easy for me? Just accept it. You get divorce papers drawn up however you want, and I'll sign them."

"Divorce?" Her voice echoed in her ears, bounced off the walls, off the ceiling, off the air, off the floor. She stared at him. A storm gathered speed in her head, turning her thoughts into a tornado. She couldn't think. Couldn't comprehend.

He turned away. "Wait." She choked and coughed. "Tell me what's going on. I don't understand. Where are you going?"

He walked through the kitchen to the garage. She watched his back the whole way. "Where are you going? Have you talked to Peter and Julie?" He shut the door quickly, noisily, firmly. She heard the garage door open, his car back out and surge forward. The sound of the engine grew faint.

Sometime later, she was still staring at the door he'd walked out of when the phone rang and jolted her out of a daze. It was Sadie, the Presbytery's Pastor to Pastors. She was coming over.

Wind and laughter blew into the house with Peter and Julie who had Wolfie in tow. Suzanne called to them from the dining room. "Come, sit down. We need to talk. Have you seen your dad today?"

"No, he was still asleep when we left," Peter said as he and Julie sat down in their usual places at the table. "Is something wrong?"

"He was here a few minutes ago." Suzanne said. "He said …. He said he's leaving." Wolfie stood at her side up on his hind legs, pawing at her leg until she picked him up.

"Leaving? Where's he going?" Peter took his coat off.

Suzanne held the dog with one arm and with the other rubbed her forehead. "I don't know what's happening. Something must have gone wrong at church."

Julie crossed her arms. "If he's leaving his church, there's no way I'm moving just before my senior year. And, Mom, you can't leave. You've just started at that church."

"Why would Dad leave? Isn't this his dream church?" Peter asked.

"I don't know. I can't think. Sadie called. She'll be here in a few minutes. Maybe she knows more." Sadie had been a good friend of the family ever since she helped Suzanne deal with gossip in her last church in Middletown, and she'd stayed close to the family when Peter had his accident.

"I'll make tea," Julie said at the same time Peter said, "I'll make coffee." They giggled. Suzanne heard them, but nothing penetrated the buzzing force field which surrounded her.

* * *

Twenty minutes later Sadie sat down with them at the table after sharing hugs all around and accepting a cup of coffee. "I'm so sorry," she said.

"We don't know what's going on." Julie lifted her hands in the air and let them fall, banging on the table.

Sadie took a deep breath. "What did your dad tell you?"

"He hasn't talked to the kids," Suzanne said, "and I don't understand what he told me. I'm guessing something happened at church to upset him, and when he settles down, he'll be back to tell us about it."

"He should have explained everything to all three of you." Sadie sat straight and tall, looking official in her usual navy suit and white shirt. She set a file folder on the table, wiped her eyes and then set her jaw. "It's not fair of him to leave it up to me."

"You're all we have," Suzanne said. "Tell us what you know."

"You and I should talk in private first," she said.

"No, whatever it is, we all need to know."

"I guess there's no help for it." Sadie slumped. "Everything will be announced in church tomorrow." She closed her eyes and said, "Lord God, give me the words; let us all feel your arms holding us and holding us up." She sipped her coffee then took a deep breath.

Julie moved her chair back as if she were about to be attacked. Peter folded his arms across his chest like Bell often did. Suzanne moaned and shifted the sleeping Wolfie.

"I want to emphasize that your father should be telling you this, but I believe he has left town, and rather than your hearing gossip, I'm going to tell you the truth. It will be difficult to hear. But then I'll answer any questions you have—if I know the answers.

"Two months ago we received a letter in the presbytery office from a woman accusing Bell of misconduct. A week later another woman wrote a similar letter." She looked each of them in the eyes. "That set in motion a process we have in place. An investigative committee was appointed to determine if the charges had validity. It was made up of well-respected elders and ministers from churches in our presbytery. You wouldn't have known about it unless Bell told you. It's a highly confidential process. They found the charges were sufficient to hold a church disciplinary trial, and they set about to arrange that. In such a trial there are precautions to guarantee fairness to everyone involved. The charges are presented and then the defense responds. Instead of going through the disciplinary process, Bell decided not to fight it. He renounced the jurisdiction of the church. That means he gave up his ordination and cannot be a pastor any more in the Presbyterian Church. He had other options, but that was his choice, so the matter died. But of course he had to leave his church and ...."

"And his family?" Suzanne said, standing up. "This can't be happening."

"What kind of misconduct?" Julie asked.

Suzanne sucked in a breath and grabbed the edge of the table. "Sexual misconduct?"

Sadie nodded.

"But that's not Bell. He's never ... he's not .... I mean he's always been so awkward socially and when it comes to intimacy on any level. I don't know how he could ...." She slumped back down in the chair and stared at the table without seeing.

Peter turned to his mother. "It doesn't fit. He's never been comfortable with anybody but you."

Suzanne jerked her head up. "Wait, he'll be back. He hasn't taken anything with him."

Sadie thought a minute. "You'd better check your joint bank accounts. And there may be things in the house you haven't noticed missing."

"Maybe he left a note," Peter said jumping up from the table. "Julie, check the dining room and living room." He ran upstairs.

They came back to the kitchen. "His clothes are gone," Peter said.

Julie wiped away tears. "Why wouldn't he at least leave a note for me ... and Peter?" She called his mobile phone. It rang in the living room. She found it stuffed down in his favorite chair. "Mom, have you seen the cats?"

"No."

"I think he took our cats with him ...."

"But not us," Peter whispered.

Chapter 11

Sadie called Dave and offered to meet with the session before church and to preach for them on Sunday. And she called Peter and Julie's partners in their day camp business. She made it possible for all three of them to be relieved of responsibilities for as long as they needed. At their request she asked people to give them a time of privacy to recover from a great shock.

The first few days they moved about the house in slow motion, trying out theories on each other, staring at the walls. They found Bell had taken half their savings, some clothes, the cats, and his car, but nothing else. Julie wondered if some gang had threatened to harm his family or his church if he didn't go along with them. Peter said he was probably abducted by aliens, and one of them had been impersonating their dad the last few days. Then more seriously, he said, "If I'd played football like he wanted me to, this wouldn't have happened."

They ordered pizza, Chinese, anything to keep from going out of the house. The kids ate, but Suzanne had no appetite. Her stomach rebelled at everything except cheese and crackers. Her brain whirled day and night, trying to fit together the pieces of her broken mind and heart. The first two nights she couldn't sleep at all. She lay in bed numb, calling on God to be with her. When she finally did fall into an exhausted sleep, she had nightmares. In one the family was hiking when Bell fell off a cliff. They couldn't find him. In another she was driving. The brakes wouldn't work. The car went faster and faster until it hit a curve and drove off the road through trees and brush. She woke from these dreams soaked in sweat and crying.

* * *

Sadie preached at Lamb of God Church and communicated with them about what had happened, telling them to call her, not Suzanne, if they had any needs or questions. She talked with Suzanne every day.

"Who are the women?" Suzanne finally asked.

"You have a right to know, Suzanne. I've been waiting until you asked. One is a single woman who is not a member of the church. I don't know her, but her name is Joy White. The other one who filed a complaint is Pamela Sorbonne."

Suzanne gasped. "But I know Pam. We taught the kindergarten Sunday school together. How could she?"

Sadie was silent and then continued. "There's another woman, Ellen Foster. She volunteered in the office."

"Sadie, do you know where he is?"

"It's my understanding that he and Ellen left town together. I think they went to Colorado, but I don't know exactly where. The church office may have an address."

Suzanne paced around the kitchen as far as the phone cord would allow. "Why did so many people know about this and nobody told me?"

"I'm sorry. I know it seems that way, but in truth we followed the process and the confidentiality necessary to it. Only the five people on the investigative committee knew, and they were cautioned not to tell anyone even their spouses. Bell was free to tell whomever he wanted to, but I don't think he told anyone."

"How could I have been so blind?" she asked Sadie. "I totally trusted him. We've always operated on trust. It wasn't unusual for either of us to go to lunch or have meetings or counseling sessions with someone of the opposite sex."

* * *

Suzanne tried not to cry in front of the children, but wasn't always successful. A word, a picture, an image would bring scattered memories of Bell: That nervous first date, his joy-filled face at their wedding, his awe when Peter was born and the soft way he still looked at Julie, vacations, seminary, their support of each one's call to ministry, helping each other with ideas and advice, that first time they went to the lake with Jewell and Ed and the kids. The two of them got up early and watched the sunrise. Where did it all go? Was it all false?

Sobs broke out without warning. She couldn't control them. She turned all the pictures in the house face down. Her doctor gave her blue pills, which she took every four hours. She couldn't sleep at night without them. They left her groggy, but she could function during the day.

One day Julie asked, "Have you told Grandmother and Granddad?"

It had been five days. Suzanne hadn't called anyone. At first she was sure Bell would come back and explain it all. Surely, he'll write or call, she thought. For sure, he'll arrange to see the kids before school starts, before Peter goes away.

Finally, she called her mother and father and asked them both to get on the phone. They were shocked. Her father kept saying, "I never would have thought it of him." Her mother wanted her to come home so she could take care of her.

"Mom, I don't think I can handle the anxiety I feel when I'm out of my own home. Maybe later. I know it seems like I should be able to, but even the travel is more than I can think about. Let me get my feet under me and I'll see. I need to go back to work as soon as I can. Keeping this job is more important than ever. Anyway, taking care of other people and keeping busy might help."

"You don't deserve to be treated like this, Suze," her mother said, crying so hard she had to get off the phone.

Each of her sisters called her. The youngest, Rebecca was a nurse. "Has he had a bump on the head? A brain injury can cause someone to act out of character like this."

Melanie had a friend who handled a similar situation with grace. "She said she slept better than ever without his snoring, and she used the other side of the bed to lay her clothes out for the next day."

Elizabeth said God had a purpose and a plan. "You're a strong woman. You'll be better off. This is a gift from God."

"No!" Suzanne cried. "God didn't make this happen. People don't always act the way God would have them act."

"No, of course not. You're right. We're all torn up about this. You've always been the one we've looked up to. Why you practically raised us. I've always seen you as God's favorite, and I'm struggling with how to think about this and what to say. Suzanne, I'm so sad that you've been hurt. All I know is you've modeled for us younger ones how to be a strong woman. Peter and Julie will watch how you manage this. You'll show them that they can handle whatever life brings them."

She called Frances. Every phone call, every person she talked with made it more real. Saying aloud what happened cut into her heart. However, her need for support outweighed her pain.

"Frances, something awful has happened."

"What is it? Peter?"

"No, he's fine, not even having to take seizure medication anymore."

"Tell me."

"It's Bell. He's left." She couldn't go on. Sobs escaped and wouldn't stop.

"Left?"

"He's left us and his church. He's run away," she managed to say.

"Suzanne, I can't hear you very well. Did you say he's run away?"

"Yes. He's left everything. We don't even know where he is."

"What happened?"

Suzanne took a deep breath. "He ... he ...."

"Oh, no. Another woman?"

"Three. He wouldn't even go through the disciplinary process of the church to defend himself. He renounced the jurisdiction of the church and gave up his ordination. Frances, I can't stand this. I can't stand it. I'm coming apart at the seams." She sobbed and then was overcome with the hiccups.

"Suzanne, I am so sorry, so sorry. I want to talk with you more but I have someone coming in the door—an appointment—counseling. Hang in there. I'll call back later and we can talk. Okay?"

"Sure," Suzanne said. But the comfort she expected to feel collapsed in her aching chest.

While she waited for the call, she joined Julie and Peter in front of the television, but her mind kept wandering and her eyes glazed over. At nine-thirty Frances still hadn't called. She felt a wave of tears start in her stomach and move up into her chest. Before they could take over, she said good night to the kids and took a pill on her way to bed. Wolfie followed her.

* * *

Julie knocked softly. "Mom?"

"Yes, Julie?"

"I saw your light was still on. I brought you a cup of tea."

Wolfie barked in his sleep, then snuggled closer to her and continued snoring as Julie tiptoed in and handed Suzanne the cup.

"Thanks, babe," Suzanne said as she put down her journal and pulled her feet up to give Julie room to sit down.

"Mom, are you going to be okay?"

Suzanne felt tears gather. "I will if you will, sweetheart."

"But I don't know how to help," Julie said. "This is so awful for you."

Suzanne set the tea on the nightstand, and gave Julie a hug. "I've been trying to get myself together so I can be both mother and father to you and Peter."

"Did I hear my name?" Peter said, coming into the room. "Is this a private party?"

"Come in, Peter," Suzanne said. "We're trying to figure out how to take care of each other."

"I'm the one who should be taking care of you," he said. "Man of the house and all that."

"No, no, that's not fair. I hate it when people say that to boys. It's a terrible responsibility they can't fulfill. Of course, you're more than a boy, but still ...."

"I've decided to put off going to college for another year. I can stay here and help you two. We're going to need extra money, too. I can earn some to help out."

The phone rang.

"It's not Frances. It's Loretta," Julie said.

"Okay. You two get ready for bed while I talk with Loretta a few minutes? Then we can think about this some more."

"Suzanne, I'm sorry to bother you. I hope it's not too late, and I know we're not supposed to call. Sadie said to call her with anything, and I did, but she said it was okay to call you with this. But tell me, are you going to be okay? We've all been so concerned. And, honey, we've been praying for you to be strong in spite of this shitty treatment. Several of us have been there so .... Sorry, I'm rambling on, I guess I'm a little nervous about calling you."

"Loretta, it's okay. Tell me, how is everybody at church?"

"We're getting by. Sadie's going to preach again Sunday and

the elders are handling everything else, but what I called about is Emma. You know who she is? Sits with May in church and always wears a hat to cover her bald head."

"Yes, I know her."

"Well, she died this morning, died in her sleep, bless her heart, and I need to know what you want us to do. Not sure who to call or if you'd want to take care of it. The funeral home is waiting for me to tell them. They want the service on Wednesday. She has two sisters who are handling everything."

"Such a sweet woman. I'm sorry to hear this. Let's see. Sadie will handle Sunday, and then I can be there Monday to meet with the funeral director and the family."

"Oh my, that's a relief. I'll let them know. People are upset about Emma and I think more so because they are upset about your ... um, your life being dumped upside down. They will be glad to know you're all right .... I mean, you're ..., you know."

"Loretta, I will pull myself together. I think I'll feel better if I get busy and back to a regular schedule. Thanks for being there for me and taking care of this. Anything else going on that I need to know about?"

"No, not really. I'll catch you up to date next week. Meantime, you rest and take care of yourself, you hear? We all love you."

"Thanks, Loretta. Bye for now."

***

Peter sat with his legs over the arm of the chair while Julie lounged across the bed, and Suzanne sat cross-legged, drinking her cold tea.

"Let's talk about how we're going to handle this," Suzanne said. "No one of us can take care of the other two. It's a huge loss for each of you as well as for me." She closed her eyes and wrinkled her forehead, trying to think how to proceed. "Those counsellors the Presbytery has arranged for us will be helpful, I think. Julie, you can go ahead and make an appointment with yours—she's here in town. Peter, Sadie says you okayed having the pastor in Winfield be yours, so you can start with him as soon as you want to when you get there." He started to speak, but she held up her hand. "Let's assume for now that you will begin college as planned. They've arranged a pastoral counsellor at Prairie View for me. It's on the way home from my church, so I can make an appointment right away. That's one way we can get support. Of course, we will hold each other up, too. And we can pray. I know there are many people praying for us. Don't forget, God works in many ways."

"Sarah and Matthew are keeping up the playground work and waiting to come over until we give the go ahead," Julie said. "And I think their mom and dad want to come, too. They're like family. They want to be with us. And they haven't seen Wolfie since your birthday party. We should invite them soon. And Frances, what about her? She's always been your best friend."

"What would help me is to find Dad and punch him in the face," Peter said, and they all laughed.

"Yeah," Julie said. "That might feel real good, but I'd settle for yelling at him. Mom, what about you?"

"Hmmm. I want to shake him by the shoulders until he talks. We deserve an explanation. If we're going to be split apart, I need to know why. But it's looking like that's not going to happen."

"I need to decide about college," Peter said. "I can wait a year. It might be easier for everybody if I do."

"Would it make life easier for you, Julie?"

"No, not really, as long as we talk a lot and you come home every chance you get."

"Yes, that's true for me, too, Peter. I'm thinking it wouldn't necessarily make life easier for Julie and me although we're going to miss you something terrible," Suzanne said. "You need to do what's best for you. Finances may not be better if you wait. You can't count on the college offering you the same scholarships next year. It's going to be hard to work through all this, but we need to get on with our lives and retool them to operate—without, without your dad around."

"He wasn't ever here, even when he was here," Peter said.

"God is our true father," Julie said. "He will protect us and show us how to live, and we should pray for Dad. Remember about God weaving everything together for good."

Pray for him? Suzanne thought. I keep hoping he'll come back. That's my prayer. Surely it's God's will that he will come back, we'll be a family, and we'll all have our lives back.

Chapter 12

FRANCES called early the next morning. "Suzanne, I'm so sorry I didn't get back to you last night. I'll explain later, but right now, tell me what you need. Do you want to talk, do you want me to come be with you? Do you need to come here?"

"I'm not sure what I need. Can't think. I get overly anxious even going to the grocery store. I'm calmer in the house, but I just sit and stare. No energy."

"I understand. It's a terrible shock. What did Bell tell you?"

"Not much. He said he was leaving his life and starting a new one. And he told me to get divorce papers ready. I keep trying to figure this out. Maybe I was controlling like he said. Could it be I didn't support his ministry enough? Nothing makes sense. We have two children, the lights of our lives. Our marriage wasn't perfect but no one's is. It was good, very good. You know us better than anyone. Tell me what you see. Was I blind to his needs?"

"No, Suzanne, as far as I can see there was nothing like that. Of course, nobody sees what's actually going on with a couple."

"Did you ever see such a tendency in Bell? I can't imagine him .... He's so socially awkward, charismatic in the pulpit but not dealing on an intimate level in conversation with individuals. If I could figure out what the truth is ...."

"You're looking for truth?"

"Yes, maybe the truth will set me free."

She was silent for a long time. "Did he ever tell you why he left Columbus Social Services?"

"Fund raising wasn't his thing; they needed an executive who could do that."

Silence lasted three beats.

"Tell me."

"I had to get permission to tell you. That's one reason I didn't call back last night. You remember Sylvia, the secretary in the office?"

"Not her, too!"

"When the board found out, they fired both her and Bell."

"Why didn't you tell me? I had no idea."

"It was a difficult decision. I was sworn to secrecy. But mostly I wanted what was best for you, and I thought maybe it was a one-time thing. Now that I know it wasn't, I'm really sorry I didn't find a way to warn you."

"I wonder how many others."

"I don't know of anyone else."

"How could he do this to me? He never indicated he was unhappy. He never complained except when I told him he was drinking too much. We saw eye to eye on so much; that's why we were attracted to each other. All this time, was he seeing life so differently from the way I was? Maybe if I had given up my calling to be a pastor and stayed home, it would have made his life easier, but time and again he supported my work and was concerned about my safety. Besides I've been a stay-at-home mom these past few years since Peter's accident. I don't get it. I never doubted that he loved me although he was never very affectionate. It was his nature ... I thought.

"Frances, what am I going to do? I don't think I can stand this. I feel like I'm dried up and withered at the roots. My life is over, cursed like the failed fig tree in the Bible. I don't know how to go on."

"Your fig tree will blossom again. But let me ask you this. Are you suicidal?"

After a long pause, Suzanne whispered, "Maybe." Am I, she wondered? "It has crossed my mind. This hurts so bad."

"Thinking of how?"

"Frances," she sobbed. "I don't how to make this better. But no. No, I could never do that to my kids."

"Hang in there. Hang in there. Call me if you ever get that low. Promise me."

"Yes. Yes, I will. Tell me how the man I've known all this time could do such a thing to me and to himself."

"I know, I know. Remember when Chet and I went through a rough patch, when he was attracted to that woman?"

"Yes."

"I remember Bell saying maybe Chet was justifying it somehow. I wonder if he said that because it was how he handled such a thing himself. Didn't you try to get him to go to a counsellor?"

"Yes, several times. He never would go. He'd be more attentive for a while. Maybe I should have been more insistent. Surely I could have done something differently. This is so sad, so sad. All those years we've been together. Now I don't know what was real and what wasn't. My mind goes in circles."

"It is sad, Suzanne, and I'm so sorry this has happened. It's not fair. It's just not fair. And I'm so angry I could spit. Do you and the kids want to come here for a while?"

"No, thank you. I get anxious when I'm outside the house. However, I am going back to work on Monday, funeral on Wednesday. I think getting busy may help. The kids are going to go back to their jobs, too."

"What do you need from me?" Frances asked.

"Please pray for us. We have to be able to go on."

Chapter 13

The clock showed 4:30 a.m. Suzanne turned over again, much too early to get up. Her thoughts raced. What if I cry at the funeral home? What do I know about Emma? I could call May and ask her to tell me what she'll remember about Emma. Have I met any of her family? Did Loretta say they wanted a service at the church or at the funeral home? What will I wear today? I should try to sleep more, or I will be too tired to drive home later.

Finally, unable to fall back to sleep, she got up and took one of the blue pills the doctor had prescribed. By the time she dressed, it had calmed her down. I must ask the doctor if I'm getting too dependent on those, but I do need them to keep me from falling apart. Over coffee and toast, she wrote down all her worries in a list and at the bottom, "God help me." But she was too restless to pray or even be still before God.

At the church she took Wolfie out of his car carrier, held him in one arm, hitched her book bag and purse over the other shoulder, and carefully took one step at a time down the steep steps into the basement.

As she reached the last step, she realized Melba was watching. "I heard you weren't coming back."

"Who said that?"

"I was told that woman from the Presbytery said you weren't

going to be a pastor any more. We thought somebody new was coming this morning."

Suzanne shook her head and took Wolfie to her office where he crawled into his little home. She wanted to throw something. Melba was right behind her. "Divorced people can't be pastors, can they?"

Suzanne didn't trust herself to say anything. She nodded and Melba went back to her office. Her heart beat persistently fast, and her breath kept pace with it. She felt tears gathering, but her attention was drawn to notes on her desk.

Loretta had left a map to Chisholm Trail Funeral Home with the time of her appointment with the family. There was also a note from Eileen and directions to her house, asking her to stop by that morning after she finished talking with Emma's sisters.

The funeral home was a short drive north, then west from the church. Suzanne passed a weedy lot next to a decrepit shack and several auto sales and repair stores. In another section, truck cabs littered a field. Then the roads narrowed. Trailers and old, sterile-looking apartments lived next to each other. She turned on Chisholm Road. On the corner sat The Bordello Club, which had pictures of dancing women across its low slung roof. On down the road, a sign in front of Long's Drug Store proudly proclaimed that in the 1800's this was a stop on the Chisholm Trail. To Suzanne the street looked like an old Western town from a cowboy movie. There were no sidewalks, and stores on either side sat close to the road. Some buildings looked empty, but a few cars sat in front of the drug store as well as a laundromat and a café.

Between the drug store and laundromat, a sign over a narrow door identified The Chisholm Mortuary. No Victorian house for a funeral home here. The two-story red brick structure sat stiffly packed into its space. She tried the door, which was locked.

Her hands shook. She searched for the blue pills. She wasn't due for one, but any anxiety left her short of breath and teary. Before she could decide whether to take one, she heard a key in the lock on the other side of the door. A lanky man with a gray handlebar mustache fit right into the scene behind him—a horsehair divan facing a fireplace, which had a rifle hanging above it, and a spittoon on the hearth.

This is like one of those crazy dreams I have, Suzanne thought. Maybe I'm asleep.

"Hello, I'm Suzanne Hawkins, pastor for Emma Conway. Is the family here?"

"Yes, Pastor, I'm Will James. My sister Lil and I are here to serve you." He bowed and instead of shaking her hand, held the tips of her fingers. She wouldn't have been surprised if he'd kissed them. "Come right in. I'll show you to the parlor. This is your first time here, I believe. We have a parlor on the alley. You can park back there next time."

The musk of old wood grew stronger as he led her through a long hallway toward the back of the building. A faint rendition of "Nearer My God to Thee" filled the solemn air. They passed several closed doors on their left and their right, but one open door revealed a sparse office where a gray-haired woman typed rapidly on a computer.

The end of the hallway opened into what looked like a modern living room, not at all in keeping with the western décor at the front. It even had a picture window which looked out onto the alley. Heavy, red velvet drapes covered all but a center portion, which let in some light. In front of the window, with their backs to it, were two women who looked down into an open casket.

"Frannie and Laura, this is Reverend Hawkins who'll be doing the service for Emma." They acknowledged Suzanne, and she moved to stand beside them. They all looked at the waxen face and tightly curled gray hair, an obvious wig covering Emma's bald head instead of her usual hat.

"I'm sorry for your loss, Frannie and Laura," Suzanne said.

"I haven't known Emma very long, but I called on her shortly after I arrived at the church."

"Let me tell you right off that we don't want anything personal in the service," Laura said. "We've all been clear about that for some time."

"That's fine. I can do that. Was she the oldest of you three?"

"Yes," Frannie said. "I'm next and Laura's the youngest. We'd like a simple graveside service on Wednesday."

"Yes," Will said to Suzanne, "at ten in the morning over at Calvary Methodist Church near Valley Center."

"That's right," Frannie said, pulling her handkerchief out of her sleeve. "They have a little cemetery beside the church. She was married in that church and her Amos is buried there. We want a simple service, nothing personal. Read the twenty-third Psalm and whatever you usually do."

"Yes, I can do that."

There was an awkward pause. "Had Emma been sick?" Suzanne asked.

"No, at least if she was she never told anyone," Laura said putting her arm around Frannie. "She died in her sleep. We should all be so lucky."

"Tell me about her life," Suzanne said.

Frannie obliged, "We grew up on a farm west of here. When Mama died, Emma was twelve. I was nine, and Laura was seven. Emma became our little mama."

"What will you remember about her?"

"She liked cats," Frannie said.

Laura interrupted. "Don't tell that. People will think she was a crazy cat lady."

"No, nothing personal. I promise. But I'd like to know more about her as we celebrate her life."

Will broke in, "Ladies, are you ready to open the drapes?"

When they nodded, Will drew open the drapes in front of the

casket revealing the whole window. The women moved to the side so he could wheel Emma up against the window. "Pastor," he said, "we do this so people can drive through the alley back here and pay their respects."

O, my God, they have a drive-through mortuary, Suzanne thought. I really am in a dream.

"I guess we're finished here," Laura said. "We'll see you on Wednesday."

Suzanne drove to Eileen's house on the way back to the church, all the while replaying in her head the visit with Emma's family. I didn't pray with them. Did I miss the moment to do that? They seemed to simply want a functionary to get the burial done. I wonder if she's actually a member at Lamb of God. If she's being buried at the Calvary Methodist Church cemetery, I'd better be sure she isn't a member there. If she is, I'll be stepping on somebody's toes.

* * *

Dave and Eileen's house sat at the end of a long gravel drive. The roof line spread out long and low. It sloped down over a porch which stretched all the way across the front. That's a genuine ranch style, Suzanne thought.

Neighboring houses could barely be seen through bushes and trees on three sides of the house. Around Lamb Of God Church, lots were small, but here further from the interstate highway, there were fewer houses, larger plots of land, and even a few barns and some cattle. Dave and Eileen even had a field of wheat, unusual in this dry part of the state. It stretched out from the house to the levee, golden and ripe, almost ready for harvest.

Suzanne pulled herself out of the car and put a smile on her face wondering what Eileen wanted.

"Suzanne, come in," Eileen said as she held the door open. "I hope the meeting with Emma's sisters went well. They're a little different. This way," she said, leading her to the kitchen.

The living room furniture had curvy legs and gold and white trim. As they walked through, Eileen paused and pointed out a family photo on the wall. "These are my boys fooling around last Fourth of July in the back yard."

In the picture the two young men wore cowboy hats, and they were laughing as they hoisted a bench holding their mother and father. Dave smiled brightly, and Eileen pursed her lips. The boys had their dad's grins and muscles. There were no pictures of the daughter Dave was searching for. Suzanne reminded herself Dave had asked her not to mention Liz to Eileen.

In the kitchen, Suzanne sat at the table, which held the leavings from a meal. "Sorry," Eileen said. "Let me move this out of your way. I thought I'd have it cleaned up before you got here. My boys stop by for lunch when they can. Want a cup of coffee? Let me see if there's still some. Yes. How about it?"

"Sure. Thanks, Eileen. I saw your note asking me to stop on my way back to the church."

"Yes, I fixed some food for you. So sorry to hear about the troubles. But, you know, no one in the church is going to look down on you. It's not your fault. Some men …. Loretta's been there. She can tell you all about how she got through it."

While Suzanne drank her coffee, Eileen pulled food out of the refrigerator and put it in a cooler. "This will keep 'til you get home," she said. "Just a little to help you through the next week. There's lasagna on the bottom, a gelatin salad on top of that, some green beans, and a couple of desserts. Freeze what you don't want now."

"How thoughtful of you. Thanks. Thank you so much."

Eileen sat down at the table with Suzanne. "How're you holding up, dear?"

"I'm doing okay, I guess. Will you tell me what was said in church the last two Sundays?"

"You mean about those black people?"

"What?"

"Three blacks came to church."

"Is that a problem?" Oh, Lord, she thought, help me know what to say and what not to say.

"If Brenda had been there, she'd have ushered them out and told them where the black church is, but nobody said anything ... except Dave, that is. He knew one of them and was friendly. That husband of mine! I wish he hadn't done that. They came back again yesterday. I hope somebody tells them where their church is." Eileen's lips pursed into disapproval almost covering those buck teeth of hers. Lord, have mercy, Suzanne thought. "But if you didn't know that," Eileen went on, "what were you asking me about?"

"I'm wondering what was said about me?"

"Let's see. The woman from Presbytery used some long words, but it added up to your husband done something wrong and left his church, and she asked us to pray for you."

"What did she say about when I'd be back?"

"The first week she said she'd be coming on Sundays until you came back and the second week, yesterday, she said you'd be back Monday, today."

"Nobody said I was quitting?"

"Heavens, no. Is somebody spreading rumors? If they are, you can bet they're coming from Melba. She'd like nothing better than for you to fail. She probably thinks Norm would come back. But if he did, we'd have to put up with Brenda. I don't know if you've been told that Melba and Brenda have been real close ever since childhood." Suzanne shook her head, and Eileen continued. "Evidently they grew up in the same town. I don't know the whole story, but they've always been real tight."

* * *

Suzanne walked into the church ready to confront Melba about who said she wasn't coming back. But Melba was on the phone, the radio was blaring, and a fan on her desk added to the noise. So Suzanne turned toward her own office and checked for messages.

Later—she didn't know how much later—she realized she had been standing at her desk staring without seeing. Snapping out of it, she reached down to pick up Wolfie from his cage. He wasn't there. The door stood open. Did I close it when I left? Did I bring him this morning? If I left him at home, will Julie and Peter notice and take him outside and feed him? Maybe I brought him but left him in the car all this time. Her mind spun like a top.

Then she noticed Melba waving to her from across the room. She hung up the phone and pointed to her lap. In seconds Suzanne stood in front of her little pup who was curled up and sound asleep on Melba's lap.

"Melba, I'm so glad he's okay. I didn't know where he was." A tear plopped onto her hand.

"He's fine. I thought he might like to sit with me a while," she said. Her face had lost its pinched look, and she even smiled. "I had a dog once. His name was Mike. But my dad gave him away. Brenda was allergic to him."

"You mean Norm's wife Brenda?"

"Yes, she lived with us."

Wolfie woke up and looked around. It seemed to Suzanne that those huge eyes saw everything that was going on and knew more than anyone suspected. She pulled the soft, furry pup to her chest, and he nestled his head under her chin. Melba's eyes followed him.

"I didn't realize you'd known Brenda that long," Suzanne said.

"Yes. We grew up a ways west of here. When her dad died, my parents took her in."

The phone rang. It was Loretta. Suzanne went back to her office to take the call, cradling Wolfie like a baby. "Loretta, I was about to call you."

104

"How are you, Suzanne? Did you find the funeral home without trouble?"

"Yes, thanks for the map and directions. There will be a short graveside service on Wednesday at a Methodist Church near Valley Center. And they want it private, so we don't need to get word to the congregation."

"I'm not surprised," Loretta said. "They're very private people. Emma wasn't, but she doesn't get a say now. They can do what they want. She was a sweetheart, and I'll miss her. God rest her soul."

"Loretta, tell me what was said in church when I wasn't here – I mean about what was going to happen."

"Sadie said your husband had crossed ethical boundaries and had left the church. She said she'd be here on Sundays until you came back. Then yesterday she told us you'd be back today. Is that what you mean?"

"Yes, exactly. I heard some conflicting reports. One was that people thought I wasn't coming back at all."

"Well, they didn't hear that in church. And I haven't heard any rumors, not even a question that sounds like that. Somebody made that up out of thin air."

"That's a relief. Thanks."

That over, Suzanne turned her attention to planning sermons and looking ahead at the church calendar. There was also a stack of mail that had to be dealt with. She was deep in concentration when she heard Melba turn off the radio.

"Melba, I didn't realize it was so late. I've checked out the rumors you mentioned. No one else has heard them, so I guess all we need to do is be clear that I will be here for the foreseeable future. If you know anyone who wondered, you could call and tell them that. Refer any questions to me."

Melba was halfway up the stairs before Suzanne stopped speaking. She simply said a terse, "Okay, bye."

CHAPTER 14

On Tuesday Suzanne stayed home to plan the service for Emma and work on her next sermon. On Wednesday, following the brief graveside service and several hours in the office, Suzanne left for her first appointment with the counsellor who had agreed to see her through this crisis. She kept taking deep breaths, trying to calm herself as she drove from the church north on I 135 to Newton. It was a twenty minute trip to Prairie View, where she would meet him. *I shouldn't have scheduled this on the day of a funeral—too much for one day. The blue pills aren't giving me as much relief as they did at first.*

That morning's service had been short and sweet. Only five people attended. But that's what Emma's sisters wanted. The only time Suzanne felt anxious was trying to find the church. But that eased as soon as she drove up. The pastor, whom she had called, came out to meet her and again thanked her for checking to be sure Emma wasn't a member of that church.

She tried to calm her racing heart as she left the lofted interstate and followed a local road east from Newton. Now, rather than sitting high above the fields, she sat close to the prairie, which stretched out on both sides of her toward the horizon. Little bluestem grasses clumped, their bright green stalks beginning to show a hint of blue. The big bluestem had shot up, its stems waving some in the wind though they stood far shorter than their tall fronds to come. She imagined pioneers riding their horses across this prairie. Someone had told her the grasses grew so tall you couldn't see a man on a horse.

A sign to Prairie View Mental Health Center pointed down another road to the south. She drove along slowly with the windows down, soothed by the wind rippling through the grass. Then, over a rise, an oasis appeared: soft green lawns and large trees. She drove along a curved driveway, following signs to the administration building, and crossed over a small stream. Weeping willow trees hung down over it. Oaks and maples and a crab apple tree stood closer to the main building. Such large trees were noticeable and surprising in Kansas. In the early days wood was so scarce settlers used limestone for fence posts.

She parked near the entrance and left Wolfie in his carrier under an oak tree before going in. A pleasant young woman welcomed her, told her Dr. Bill would be with her soon, and gave her folders describing the facility. She read that there were acres of natural prairie on the land in addition to the manicured center of the campus. Buildings included a gym and a pottery workshop, an inpatient hospital, rooms for group therapy, offices, and two large classrooms for workshops and retreats. Several events listed for clergy in the next months looked interesting. A second folder detailed the history of the center. It was begun in 1954 by the Mennonite Church to provide more humane treatment for people who suffered from mental illness. More recently it had expanded to offer family therapy and to serve those with addictions.

When she sat, Suzanne's legs bounced nervously as though she'd had too much caffeine, so she walked around trying to calm herself and looked out the window to check on Wolfie. It was hot and she needed to find a cooler place for him. She turned to ask the young woman at the desk, but as she did so, a man with twinkling eyes started toward her.

She liked him immediately. He looked like Jean Luc Picard,

a perfectly oval hairless head and deep brown eyes. He had that air of a strong, but gentle, man.

When he heard about Wolfie, he encouraged her to bring him in and hold him while they talked. That helped remove one level of her anxiety. They sat down at a round table in his office. Wolfie was cooperative and calm, easy to take places since he rarely barked at people. They talked nonstop, and Suzanne's anxiety lessened greatly. She left, hopeful that here she could find help.

Later, at home she took a short nap until Peter and Julie came home from their long day entertaining children at the playground. Matthew and Sarah came in with them, and soon their parents arrived as well. Jewell and Ed had been wanting to bring dinner, and she hated to put them off any longer, although what she really needed was low stress time and more hours to sleep. But these good friends simply want to do something to help, she thought. And Suzanne found herself hungry for the first time in a long time when Jewell put potato salad and a ham on the table and promised her famous caramel cake for dessert.

"What's Robert up to tonight," Suzanne asked. "Surely he'd be here if he knew you made caramel cake."

"He's at the church," Ed said. "His work with domestic abuse has expanded beyond anything we'd have believed when he started that first center right after college. He said to give you a hug."

"What an amazing young man. You can be proud of him. And Matthew and Sarah, of course. All three of your children are outstanding human beings," Suzanne said.

She told Peter and Julie and the Edwards a little bit about Prairie View and the counseling appointment. Peter asked her if Dr. Bill said, "Make it so!" like Jean Luc. Later that night when she called Frances, she had to explain who that was. "Oh," she said, "Star Trek. You mean Patrick Stewart?"

However, she didn't tell any of them how she cried and sobbed most of the time, not able to keep up her emotional shield when telling Dr. Bill what had happened. He listened like no one she'd ever met before. He gasped when she described the two women walking out of church. He had tears in his eyes when she described the elders surrounding her when those two went on the attack. His forehead showed puzzlement when she described Bell leaving and said she couldn't find him. His face softened when she described her fears for her children and her fierce love for them. His eyes held love and light when she admitted to thinking it would have been more reasonable for Bell to die and how at times she had wished for her own death to take away this pain. She had never before met anyone who seemed to understand everything she said and felt.

Chapter 15

On the way to work one morning in mid-June, Suzanne drove the back way to see the golden fields of wheat. Following Route 4 she drove the familiar road through Harvest and Gypsum to get to I 135. Harvest Church had been her first interim in Kansas, and she knew nearly every house she drove by. I could stop anywhere and be welcomed in, she thought. What interesting people I met in the short time I was their pastor, and now they are lifelong friends. She passed Bertha's house. They had kept in touch until lately. Suzanne kept putting off telling her what had happened. Then one day Bertha called after hearing the sad soap opera story about Bell from someone in Salina.

"Suzanne," she said, "you deserve better than that. But I know what a strong woman you are, and God is with you. I'll be watching to see what good you and He make of this."

"One thing I know," Suzanne said. "This is the worst thing that could ever happen to me, so I don't need to be afraid of anything else. Nothing could be worse. Except for losing a child. Of course, that would be worse."

* * *

The first two weeks of July heavy rain and hail pounded the fields. Fortunately, it came after the wheat was cut, a relief to all who depended on a good harvest. It seemed to Suzanne the entire county held its breath until the wheat was safely gathered in.

One Friday it rained so hard in Salina there was no day camp, so Peter and Matthew decided to go shopping for what they'd need in college. It never occurred to Suzanne that Peter would go without her. When he walked out the kitchen door to the garage, her heart felt like a rock that refused to budge.

* * *

And so the summer plodded on. Suzanne saw Dr. Bill every other week, but she grew weary of those visits. She couldn't keep her feelings at bay with him, and the ache stayed with her. He told her the waves would come less often and less strong as she went. When she asked for books to read, he hesitated.

"I can give you books, but if you think you can read yourself out of this pain, you are mistaken. Books can reassure you, tell you you're not going crazy, and tell you it will get better. But you have to go through the pain. At some point you will accept that you have to give up much of the way your life was and find a way to begin a new chapter."

However, he told her she could borrow books from his shelves, and she did, reading all of them voraciously. However, he was right. They gave her knowledge, but not relief.

One day she told him, "I don't know how much longer I can go on like this. My bones are tired. In my dreams I'm so weary I can't walk. I can't stand. I'm lying on the road pulling myself along, barely able to slide forward on my stomach."

"I had no idea you were that exhausted." He rested his chin on his hand. There was a long pause, then he asked, "Are you still having nightmares?"

"Yes, it's a different scenario every night. Sometime it's like it used to be, and we're with the kids having fun, but it always ends up with him leaving. Last night he was waving a machete, and I was trying to protect the children."

"No wonder you're tired. You're working fifty hours a week and then at night going through the pain all over again. What do you want to do about that?"

"I've thought of being admitted to a hospital, resting, letting someone else make decisions; but I don't want to give someone else control over my life. I want to make the decisions."

"Could you take a week off from work?"

"Yes, I probably could, but the thought of that makes me anxious. What would I do? I need to be busy. I am better off when people need me to do something for them."

"Is there anything you're looking forward to?"

She hesitated and started to say "nothing," but after a pause, she said, "I hadn't thought about that, but I look forward to seeing where Peter is going to be, although I dread his leaving home. And in September I'll see him when I go to Winfield to the Walnut Valley Bluegrass Festival. That might be fun. But then the holidays will come ...."

"So how do you want to handle your fatigue?"

She thought about that and finally said, "I need to find a time to meditate. At one church I used to go into the sanctuary in the mornings. Yes, I could do that. It might help to start journaling my prayers again. And I'll invite some friends to go with me to the festival."

"That sounds good," Dr. Bill said. "You also need to sleep more hours than usual. Your body and your mind need rest. Next time we meet I'd like to ask you what your deepest desires are for your life. It's time for you to get clearer about who you are at your core. You can begin thinking about that if you want to or let it sit at the edge of your consciousness for now."

Suzanne felt better when she left his office that day. A ray of sunshine fell across her face, and she saw it as a sign of hope. But by the time she reached home, she couldn't remember the feeling.

It's too much, she thought. This is too much to bear. It's like someone took a knife and cut straight through me. After all these years growing together and making a home and family, he's broken a sacred covenant with me and with God. But even worse, he's abandoned his children. I don't know if I can ever forgive him for what he's doing to them. It's going to affect them as they marry and begin families. It's going to hurt them the rest of their lives.

* * *

The church was a good distraction for Suzanne. When she was working, she focused on other people. Dr. Bill noted that she often came into his office completely worn down and hopeless, but when he asked about her work at the church, she became another person, exuding confidence and the capability to do anything that came her way.

She did look forward to the weekly routine of studying the scripture lessons for the next Sunday and finding creative ways to bring the Word alive for her people. Worshipping with the congregation on Sundays brought her some joy, especially when Julie and Peter went with her.

The parishioners brought enthusiasm into the sanctuary. She noticed this because in other places she'd felt like she had to generate energy or it wouldn't be there. At Lamb of God the people lifted her up. She was especially touched to see the dedication and faithfulness of recovering alcoholics. More than one of them told her the AA meetings and Sunday worship were for them a matter of life or death. One man's occasional well-placed "Amen" encouraged and fueled her spirit.

She began reading *Alcoholics Anonymous,* which they called "The Big Book." In addition to the list of the steps, it had explanations and suggestions for each one. She began to have more understanding of what many of her parishioners had been through. Not only that, but sermons came more easily now, sermons that could apply to all of them.

Chapter 16

One morning Suzanne returned to the basement office from the sanctuary, where she had been meditating, to find Dave and Loretta waiting in her office.

"Hey, I was thinking about calling one of you." She held up *The Big Book,* which she had been reading. "I have some questions—." Seeing their somber faces, she caught herself. "But that can wait. What's going on?"

"It's Liz," Dave said, getting up to close the door. "We found her."

"You don't look like that's good news," Suzanne said.

"It's terrible—where she's living—it's filthy and drug dealers hang out on the street. And the baby ...." He couldn't go on.

Loretta filled in the gaps. "Dave kept asking people about her, and finally, for a twenty dollar bill one of them told him where to look. The baby is about four months old, and nobody's watching out for her. When we got there, Liz wasn't home, and there were people lying around stoned. None of them could even tell us the baby's name. I found the birth certificate in a pile of papers. She named her Junque."

Suzanne threw *The Big Book* on her desk. "Junk? What kind of a name is that?" She wanted to shout but was quite aware of Melba beyond her door on the other side of the radio's country music.

"She spelled it J U N Q U E," Loretta said, "as if that makes any difference."

"What are you going to do?" Suzanne asked Dave.

Looking at his feet, he shook his head slowly side to side.

Loretta spoke for him. "Dave wants to bring the baby home, but he has to get Liz's okay so she won't accuse him of kidnapping her. When we were there, she came in the door and saw her dad and about went crazy. It will take some doing to get her to agree to anything. And then there's Eileen. She probably won't accept her. The baby's not exactly white, and that won't set well with her. Don't it just break your heart?"

Dave looked up. "What do you think I should do?"

"What are your options?" Suzanne asked.

Dave looked up at the ceiling, and Loretta squeezed her eyes shut. Suzanne wrote down what they said.

- *Take her when nobody's looking.*
- *Get a lawyer involved or social services.*
- *Wait a while and go back hoping Liz will want what's best for the child.*
- *Convince Eileen to go talk to Liz.*
- *Spring the babe on Eileen. When she sees her, maybe….*
- *Let Liz figure out what to do and try to forget about it.*

Loretta stood up, hands on her hips. "I can't stand it. Who knows what might happen to her—and I won't call her 'junk' no matter how she spells it. I'm going to call her 'J', and I'm going back down there right now to have a come-to-Jesus talk with Liz." Suzanne had never seen Loretta so angry. "Dave, I think she'll be less emotional if you're not there. She and I have a long history from when I was her AA sponsor. Mark my words, I will come back with that baby. Tell Eileen or let it be a surprise—either way I'll bring her to your house. Now, let's see, I'm going to need some money."

Dave stared at her, then nodded and handed her all the bills in his wallet. Suzanne had three twenties to add.

"I'll need a car seat or …."

"Let's go," Suzanne said. "I'm going with you, and I can hold her."

Dave followed them up the steps and out the door. "You don't really think you're going to come back with the baby, do you?"

* * *

Loretta stopped at Norm's house next to the church and disappeared inside for a few minutes. "I called Billy at Mother Mary's," she explained as she jumped back in and started the engine. "He's asking Sister Johanna for the papers we need Liz to sign so she won't wake up tomorrow and accuse us of kidnapping."

Loretta sang all the way to downtown Wichita. She was keyed up.

Standing on the banks of the river, trying to get a glimpse of what's over on the other side.

Suzanne loved to hear her sing, and she joined in on the ones she knew, catching the thrill of danger and anticipation.

He touched me, He touched me, and oh, the joy that filled my soul. Something happened and now I know. He touched me and made me whole.

After they picked up the papers from Billy and Sister Johanna, Loretta said, "We're on a mission from God." She repeated it, each time louder and with more intensity. Suzanne wondered whether she was quoting the Blues Brothers or trying to screw up her courage.

"We're close now," she said as they turned onto a street with more boarded up buildings than open ones. "Suzanne, you may not want to go in when we get there. It's real disturbing."

"Do you think she's more likely to say yes to you if I'm not there?"

"I'm guessing she won't be aware enough to notice much around her."

"Then I'm going in."

Five boys stood in front of a pawn shop, smoking and laughing. The incessant Kansas wind blew food wrappers around their feet and out into the street. Loretta parked and rolled her window down. A wave of hot and humid air rolled in.

"This doesn't look good," Loretta said. "Stay in the car unless I motion you to come with me." She stepped down from the Bronco showing first those legs in their skin-tight denim, then swinging out chest high, shoulders low. The men gaped and punched each other.

"Honey," she said to the tallest one in her best Dolly impersonation, "could I get you to help me?"

They looked stunned as she strutted toward them. Suzanne felt downright dowdy, her long blond hair hanging straight and unremarkable in light of Loretta's big and showy platinum do. She sure knows her way around, Suzanne thought. Loretta showed one of the boys money, stuffed it back in her pocket, and motioned Suzanne to come with her.

They entered a street level door and climbed a narrow stairwell. It smelled like rotten potatoes. There was no sound from the apartment, which was marked with a sloppy "2."

Loretta cautiously cracked open the door. She and Suzanne stood there a moment before entering. The room had an attached kitchenette against the far wall. To the left sat a playpen with the sleeping baby. Next to that an open door revealed a toilet with the seat up. In between the entry and the kitchen, a bed, a couch, and a rug held seven bodies lounging in the unbearable heat. One boy sat shirtless upside down on the couch, legs over the top, head down and mouth open. It could have been a crime scene from a TV drama, except for the rough sounds of coughing and snoring.

"You get the baby ready," Loretta whispered to Suzanne. "I'll talk to Liz."

The young woman she pointed to sat slumped over the kitchen table, head on her arms, hair lying in a puddle of syrup which seeped out of its tipped over container.

J didn't look like a four-month-old. Her skinny arms and legs jerked, but her eyes remained closed, and she made no noise. Suzanne took her dirty diaper off and looked for another but couldn't find one. She looked in the tiny bathroom. Her stomach began to heave when she saw needles in the dirty sink and pill bottles on the floor. She quickly grabbed the least-soiled wash cloth and towel from dirty clothes thrown in the tub to clean up the baby and wrap her. She couldn't find any clothes or blankets for her.

Suzanne rocked the baby back and forth in her arms while she waited for Loretta who was speaking softly to Liz. Finally Liz held herself up on her left arm and with the other signed the paper. Then Loretta handed the bleary-eyed woman a wad of green, and they left quickly.

"There was no milk in the refrigerator, but here's a jar of baby food," Loretta said as they climbed down the stairs to the street. "Why isn't that baby crying? Do you think she's sick?"

"She hasn't been awake at all." Suzanne choked and wiped away tears. "I think she's been drugged. And she looks malnourished to me. She should be much bigger than this. Loretta, look how precious she is. How could they do this?"

"I don't know. I don't know. I doubt we'll ever see Liz again, alive anyway." She shook her head and sighed deeply. "It's so sad to see people give up. I wish I could help that girl. But right now we have this beautiful life in front of us. Look at those long eyelashes and her gorgeous color, like coffee with lots of cream. But she's going to have fits trying to tame that curly hair when she's older.

"I'll pay off these boys who watched out for my car. Then let's stop and get what we need to clean her up and dress her in a nice outfit before we introduce her to Grandma Eileen."

* * *

Suzanne became a soft pillow for the sleeping baby. She recalled her overwhelming joy when Peter and Julie were born. That led her to questions about the change in Bell, but she pushed those thoughts away and focused instead on the child in her arms, her tiny nose, little round face, and perfect lips. All the way home, Suzanne smiled as she rocked that baby back and forth and hummed "Toora-loora-looral."

After they got on the turnpike, Loretta sang it softly, "Toora-loora-looral, hush now don't you cry. Toora-loora-looral, that's an Irish lullaby."

"That was my grandmother's favorite lullaby," Suzanne whispered.

"It was? It's one of my grandmother's favorites, too," Loretta said.

* * *

By the time they drove into Dave and Eileen's street, they had fed J, cleaned her up and dressed her in a ruffled white sundress with matching bloomers. She had opened her eyes while eating, much to the delight of her rescuers, and they exclaimed over her big blue eyes.

"She will steal Eileen's heart," Loretta predicted.

* * *

Dave and Eileen sat on the porch fanning themselves. There was no way to guess what Eileen knew. Loretta jumped out first and ran up to give both of them a big hug.

Suzanne slowly followed behind, shifting J to an upright position so they could see her.

"Who's this?" Eileen asked.

"This little bundle needs someone to feed her. She needs to put on some weight," Loretta said.

You are so sly, Suzanne thought. There's no better way to get Eileen's interest.

Eileen moved toward her. "How old is she?"

"About four months," Loretta said. "Doesn't she look small for her age?"

Eileen took her from Suzanne. "Why is she so thin? Who does she belong to?" she asked Suzanne. "Look at those big blue eyes!"

"Her mother isn't able to take care of her," Suzanne said.

Eileen looked at the baby again, moved the cap and smoothed her curly black hair. "Is she black?"

Loretta looked her in the eyes and answered softly, "Half. Eileen, this baby is Liz's. She's your grandchild."

Eileen thrust the child out from her chest back to Suzanne and stared at Dave. Her eyes narrowed and her mouth pursed as she turned and stomped into the house.

Suzanne rocked the baby. "Now, now, sweetheart, you'll be okay." Maybe I could take her home—for a while, she thought. A new life, a new life. She turned to go back to the car.

The screen door banged shut and Eileen was by her side in a flash. "Here, let me have her." She grabbed the baby. "But don't ever tell my sister about her. Don't tell anyone." She rushed into the house.

"Dave, this child needs to see a doctor real soon. We think she may have been given something to keep her quiet," Loretta said. She handed him the paper Liz had signed and also the birth certificate.

Dave's jaw jumped as he clenched his teeth. "Suzanne, Eileen's sister disowned her daughter when she started dating a black man. Her whole family is quite vocal about race, but we don't have to let that affect us. We'll take good care of this baby. You can be sure of that."

Chapter 17

Dr. Bill took notes as Suzanne told him about a dream. "It seemed so real. I had a new dress, and I took the whole day off to go to a street festival. No one knew me, and I felt free from responsibility. It was fun. A band played, floats rolled by. People gathered at one corner, and I stopped there. An Episcopalian priest was serving communion. He offered the cup to each person, and when he came to me, I leaned forward to drink from the chalice, but he spilled wine all over my new dress. I was angry. It was ruined. But then the wine turned to blood. People crowded toward me, touching me. I felt powerless to protect myself; then I saw them being healed, and I felt guilty for resenting the people at first."

Suzanne sat quietly with her eyes closed until Dr. Bill spoke. "What was your primary emotion in this dream?"

"Anger at first. I was tired, so tired yet unable to get away from people needing me, and I was angry that the pastor ruined my new dress. Then I felt guilty for feeling angry. Eventually, I felt amazed and joyful to see people healed."

"And what do you see as the significance of the dream now that you are looking back on it?"

"I don't know. It doesn't make sense. It doesn't fit with who I am—I mean the blood part. I don't get the blood sacrifice, all that about shedding blood to satisfy God. That's not the God I know.

The dream doesn't sync with my theology."

* * *

Later that day she called Frances and told her about the dream.

"What does it mean to you?" she asked.

"I don't know. I've thought about it, written in my journal, talked with Dr. Bill, and I'm still nowhere. Phrases come to mind, but they're not mine: 'Washed in the blood of the lamb,' 'covered by the blood,' 'saved by the blood.'"

"What do you believe about the blood of Christ?" Frances asked.

"I don't think much about the blood. Jesus lived a life of obedience to God, a wholly faithful life, even when it cost him his life. He forgave those who wanted to destroy him because they didn't know what they were doing."

"What does it mean to you when you serve communion and say, 'This is a new covenant sealed in my blood, for the remission of your sins'?"

"He showed us what God is really like, not the terrifying, vengeful God of the Old Testament, but a loving, forgiving God who is cheering for us and hoping we will become who we were created to be, whole and creative, like God is. I think Jesus showed us how to do that, how to be sacrificial, loving servants of God and instruments of his grace. It's not about death and suffering, it's about life. A new covenant sealed with his life."

"Ah, the blood is about life." She paused. "The wine, Jesus covering you with life although that's not how you felt, so maybe I'm reading into it what wasn't there." Silent thoughts filled the moment.

"Suzanne, my spiritual director would ask what your prayer is when you're this tired."

"I pray for strength to do what is before me."

There was a long silence. Suzanne could almost hear Frances

thinking.

"A couple of questions come to mind. But I'm not sure this is a problem-solving moment, and I don't want to interfere when you have a counsellor. Maybe it's best to let this sit and settle on you for a while."

"I hate to lose what has occurred to you. I could write down your thoughts and discuss them with Dr. Bill. If they don't fit the moment, I can come back to them later."

"Yes, I know you well enough to trust that I won't throw you off track. Think about this: Are you doing what God has called you to do, or are you trying to do all of God's work, too? That's one. The other is to think about your prayer. You said you ask God to give you strength to do what's needed. I'm wondering if you have considered any other prayer."

"Those are great questions, but you're right. I can't think about them right now. I'll come back to your thoughts later. Thanks, pal. I can always count on you to understand."

When Suzanne hung up, she noticed Julie staring at her. "What was that all about?" she asked her mother.

And so Suzanne told her the dream.

"Mom, did you really dream that?"

"Yes, any thoughts on what it might mean?"

"I can't believe you dream all the stuff you've told me over the years. A lot of the time I thought you made it up like the stories you told us at night. But when I heard you talking to Frances, I realized that you wouldn't be telling her you dreamed it if you made it up."

"No, I really do have vivid dreams, and I often remember them."

"When you talk to me like you talk with her, I think you're trying to teach me something. Do you go around thinking like that all the time?"

"I'm not sure what you mean." She stared at her daughter.

How could she not know me after all these years?

"Like when you're all 'blood of Jesus' and 'will of God.' I know preachers talk like that at church, but I don't know anybody who thinks like that all the time."

"I didn't know I sounded different." Suzanne stared at a spot on the wall. "It's how I think. It's who I am."

Chapter 18

Suzanne found a pencil broken in two on her office floor one morning, and all of Wolfie's treats were gone. A few days later her sermon notes were missing but showed up in the kitchen sink. The next week Melba was holding Wolfie's carrier in the parking lot when Suzanne pulled up one morning.

"I found it back near the trash cans," she said. "We have to find out what's going on before anything worse happens."

Suzanne called Dave and left it up to him to figure it out. "Dave, I've had this kind of thing happen before in a church, and it escalated. But that was unusual. The woman was angry with God. I've heard from other pastors that mischief goes on in their churches occasionally."

The elders discussed it at their next Session meeting, and May reported similar disturbances over the years. Dave said Eileen thought it was happening because she started bringing J to worship on Sundays. No one had heard anything to indicate unhappiness about that.

May said, "It's been years since we had such a good Sunday school class. It can't be any of them. Besides, we're only here on Sunday mornings. Who has access to the building during the week?"

"AA groups are here two nights, and a new Narcotics Anonymous group has started meeting, too," Dave said. "But they all use the room behind the sanctuary. There's no reason for anyone to come down here. I'll drop in on all the meetings and see if I can figure it out. I don't like this," he said. "Of course, I'm sensitive to security since that's what I do all day at Beechcraft. We owe it to you and Melba to keep you safe. I think we ought to keep the building locked even when you women are here. We can set up a speaker and a buzzer you can press to let someone in when they tell you who they are."

Three days later a man from a security company came and walked through the building. Melba eyed him suspiciously. However, Suzanne found him quite congenial until he talked too long about his dog and his leadership role at a nearby church. When he offered Wolfie a treat, the dog turned up his nose and wouldn't look at him. "I'm sorry," Suzanne said. "I've never seen him act like that."

He installed a speaker outside the side door. During the week everyone came in and left that way, going up to the sanctuary or down to the basement. The man patiently showed Melba how to ask who it was and push a button to open the door if she chose to.

A week after the security installation, Melba found water running in the kitchen sink one morning. Another day Wolfie's crate was missing again, but this time they couldn't find it. Suzanne immediately bought another one. "I will not be distracted by this," she said to Melba. "It's not unusual for these things to happen in a church. Besides, Dave will figure out what's going on."

She sniffed. "It's probably kids or one of those alkies. They act like they own the place."

Dave had no answers. "There were no meetings here either night. I'll work this out. There has to be an answer. Let me know if anything else happens."

* * *

Suzanne kept herself going by focusing on the next sermon, the next meeting, the next person in need. Julie asked her one Sunday after church, "Mom, how can you take care of all those people and their problems—especially right now?"

"Dr. Bill asked me the same thing. I don't know. I simply put one foot in front of the other. But it's always like this in a church. I told him he was getting a glimpse into what it's like to be a pastor. Nobody knows all the troubles of those around them, but the pastor hears lots of them. It's a privilege to be considered almost one of the family when they are celebrating and also when they are hurting."

"But don't you get tired?"

"Yes, very, very tired. But it keeps my mind off my own stuff. I'll take some vacation time soon, maybe a day a week to get extra sleep. And we'll be taking Peter to school soon. That will be fun to see where he's going to be. Are you still driving with me?"

"Yes, sure," she said, but her frown remained. "We're going to need two cars to take Peter to school. One will be packed with all his stuff. Since KU doesn't start until a week later, Matthew's letting us use his car. Then when we get back to Wichita, I can drive straight to his house. The day after that we're going to Lawrence to see where he'll be living. We have it all worked out with his parents."

* * *

On the Sunday before Peter started college, the congregation celebrated with him at the fellowship time. Loretta and Eileen had hung streamers and a banner that said, "Happy, happy, happy." The table was full of food and a cake decorated by Eileen. Colorful icing balloons surrounded "Congratulations, Peter."

People patted Peter on the back and asked questions about school. The children hung around him, too, and as always he knew how to talk with them and tease them.

"He's like that at the playground," Julie said as she held J.

"A pied piper. He'll be a great dad someday."

Loretta heard them talking about taking Peter to school. "You know, you two are going to be mighty tired when you get through moving Peter into his dorm. You should come stay at my house overnight. You can leave Wolfie with me if you want to."

* * *

When the day came, Peter was ready and waiting an hour before they had planned to leave. Suzanne saw him bouncing up and down on his toes at the rear of the car and then playing imaginary drums on the trunk. He had loaded the car the night before, even filling the front seat to the roof, leaving only a small space for the driver.

Peter drove Matthew's car, and Julie went with him. Suzanne drove her over-packed car alone. She wanted to spend this time with Peter but told herself it was safer if the two of them watched the road. Anyway, if she started tearing up, it would put a damper on his mood. The brain behind her eyes sat numb as she drove on automatic.

They reached Loretta's house by ten thirty. She immediately came outside with lunches for them. "I know you all are anxious to get to school, so I won't keep you. Wolfie, you come, stay with me. I know someone who wants to hold you and feed you treats all day."

They stopped in Derby to get gas, and Julie asked to drive her mother's packed car the rest of the trip. So Suzanne rode with Peter through Mulvane and Udall to Winfield. Most of the fields around them held scrub grass, though a few acres of prairie grass waved in the wind, and in one field a sign said "milo." Gray-green dusty leaves surrounded dramatic spikes of rust-colored seeds. Hedge apple trees lined both sides of the road, bending together like a chorus line. A train leapt by on the tracks parallel to the highway. Cattle pens wound around themselves. A grain elevator sat behind a town of small houses and trailers.

"There's a red-tailed hawk," she pointed out to Peter.

"Awk, awk," he said. It brought back memories of him and Julie counting hawks on car trips.

Suzanne felt the atmosphere in the car turn from excitement to anxiety as they entered Winfield. Signs greeted them: "Bluestem Country," "Southwestern College," "Walnut Valley Bluegrass Festival." A welcoming park sat on the left side of the road.

"When Dad and I came down to see the college, we went to that park and ate our lunch," Peter said.

Suzanne's breath caught and she sighed deeply. I wonder how Peter is feeling about all this and about his father, she thought. This is the first time I've seen his jaw relax instead of tighten when he mentioned him.

In the business district, grand buildings of limestone remained from some other era. Peter turned left, and the campus lay before them. An impressive limestone building held Corinthian pillars. "Seventy-seven steps up to it," Peter said. The rest of the campus held a mix of limestone structures and low, prairie style buildings.

When they found his dormitory, a girl with hair down to her waist met them. She gave Peter a name tag the size of a plate, and pointed toward his room. Later, after an hour of carrying his belongings in the heat and humidity, they gladly unpacked boxes in the air conditioning. Peter put away clothes, Julie arranged his books, and Suzanne made his bed, smoothing out the sheets and plumping his pillow. When his roommate and his parents came in, everyone introduced themselves, and then the room seemed crowded and the moment awkward, so the families left to go back home.

"We'll be here for The Bluegrass Festival the end of September," Suzanne said, hugging him. "Have fun and learn lots."

On the drive back, Suzanne led the way, and Julie followed in Matthew's car. The only sounds were the engine droning and a fly persistently buzzing in the back window. Suzanne didn't even turn on the radio. When they pulled in at Loretta's house, Suzanne jumped out and opened the trunk to get their overnight bags, but Julie sat in the other car and didn't move to help.

Suzanne opened the car door, "Julie?"

She gripped the steering wheel and bit her lip. "I wonder where Dad is right now."

* * *

"There you are!" Loretta called out from the porch of her bungalow. "Y'all come on up here and get some lemonade." Wolfie ran down the steps and danced on his hind legs until Suzanne picked him up. She and Julie joined the three women on the porch.

"Julie, come meet my mama. Everybody calls her Mama Mary, and this is my grandmother. She's Suzanne like your mother. Everybody calls her Grand Mama. Sit, sit." She pointed to white wicker chairs, which reminded Suzanne of her grandmother's porch. "Y'all get acquainted," Loretta said. "I'll be right back. Gotta check on dinner."

"We're so glad you're here," Grand Mama said. "It gives us a chance to get to know both of you better. Seems like we never have a chance to talk since we don't stay after church on Sundays—one hour's about as much as these old bones will allow."

"I've been wanting to have some time also," Suzanne said. "I'm glad you've felt like coming to church the last few Sundays."

"Before I forget it," Grand Mama said, "I want to tell you how much last Sunday's sermon inspired me, especially that part about thinking when something good happens we're going to get hit with something bad. If we have good weather, I've been known to say, 'We're gonna pay for this.' I never for a second thought of it as assuming that God's grace is limited."

"I'm sorry I missed that," Julie said. "I was in the nursery."

Mama Mary nodded to Julie, "It sure caught my attention when you talked about how living with regret about the past and fear about the future can block the Holy Spirit."

"Can block the free flow of the Spirit," Suzanne corrected.

"Yes, yes, that's it. I'm having to think on that some more."

Loretta burst out the door. "Y'all ready for some good southern fried chicken? Mama's recipe."

"I learned from the best," Mama said. She nodded to her mother who took hold of her daughter's arm and pulled herself up. She stood a moment, then led them into the house, head held high, walking slowly but gracefully.

When they sat down at the dining room table, Suzanne realized how much the three women looked alike. They all had perfectly oval faces and beautiful soft ivory skin. Of course, Grand Mama had more wrinkles and gray hair than her daughter and granddaughter. And Loretta's big hair distracted from the similarities since the two older women wore their hair softly curled back from their faces.

"Loretta," Suzanne said, "you have prepared a feast. It all looks so good." Golden fried chicken sat in the center of the table, a gorgeous centerpiece which quickly disappeared along with the mashed potatoes, green beans, and ambrosia.

"This is delicious, Loretta," Julie said. "It reminds me of how Aunt Elizabeth makes chicken when we go see her in Alabama. Will you teach me how to cook this?"

"Why I sure will, honey. Y'all come over after church one of these Sundays, and we'll make it together."

"We come from Alabama," Grand Mama said. "Whereabouts does your aunt live?"

"Close to Decatur, I think. Is that right, Mom?"

"Yes, between Athens and Decatur, out in the country. She lives in the house where my mother grew up. It was her parents' house all their lives, too. And it's the only constant home I knew as a child. Dad was in the Air Force, and we moved a lot. So where in Alabama are you from?"

There was a pause and then all three of their hosts began talking at once. Suzanne picked out some words: "Decatur." "We're from there." "How is it possible we didn't know this?"

"What's your grandmother's name?" Grand Mama asked.

"Franny Ruth Bryan."

"My Lord in heaven," she said. Her eyes shone as though she did see the Lord in front of her. "Suzanne."

Loretta jumped up to go to her. "Are you all right?"

Grand Mama shooed her away. "Wait 'til I tell you! Wait 'til I tell you! What a grand day this is. Little Suzanne. I never, ever expected I'd see you again. Your grandmother Franny and I were best of friends all through school and ever after. When she died, I lost my best friend. She was like a sister to me. The only sister I ever had. We were that close. I knew your mother very well, too, I remember when you were born clear as if it was yesterday. The prettiest baby. You were the prettiest baby, and you're still as pretty as can be. Merciful heavens, to think that I've lived to see you again."

Suzanne's brain whirled. "You knew my mother and my grandmother? This is amazing. Are you the friend I was named for?"

"Yes, I am." Her eyes beamed even as they watered. "We discussed Suzanne or Suzanna. I'm really Suzanna, but I started telling people I was Suzanne so they wouldn't sing, 'O Suzanna, don't you cry for me. I come from Alabama with my banjo on my knee.' And so, you see, I had a hand in naming you Suzanne."

"God bless us all," Loretta said. "Here we've been connected all these weeks, and we're only now figuring it out."

"Mother sure will be surprised," Suzanne said. "When she visits, I know she'll want to see you." She paused. "Are you, by any chance, also the friend who made my baptismal dress?"

"Why, yes, I did. And I prayed for that little baby the whole time I was making it. Mary, would you hand me my Bible, it's right behind you?"

Grand Mama handed it to Suzanne. On the inside cover and fly leaf were columns of names. Hers was near the bottom of the first column.

"Grand Mama spends most of her morning with her list," Loretta said.

"I'm still praying for you every day, but I never expected to see you again. My, my, God works in mysterious ways. Would you write down your mother's phone number? I can't wait to tell her."

Julie looked from one woman to another. "This is unbelievable."

CHAPTER 19

ON Friday evening, the night before The Bluegrass Festival, Julie came home from school scowling. "Mrs. Bane used to be my favorite teacher, but not after today. She already approved my senior paper topic about subliminal advertising techniques, but then in the middle of English class, in front of everyone, she used it as an example of what she called 'lightweight' subject matter. I don't understand how she could turn on me like that."

She's feeling abandoned again, Suzanne thought. Still no word from her dad, we haven't heard from Peter in over a week, and Matthew is involved in his first months at college. So much loss for her.

* * *

"Everything has changed," Julie said, as they ate dinner in front of the television. Grief sat over and around them like a thundercloud.

Suzanne couldn't predict what bedtime would bring for her each evening. Sometimes she felt safe and comforted in God's arms. Other times she'd try to calm down by reading the Bible; though once she'd become so frustrated with the whining laments of the Psalms, she'd thrown the book across the room only to pick it up later and hold it to her tenderly. Most of the time solving a crossword puzzle satisfied her, and reading a mystery novel settled her mind.

* * *

Saturday morning they left at six heading south out of Salina to The Bluegrass Festival. The trip would take them two and a half hours. Julie's scowl still pinched her face in contrast to the sunny fall day. "Julie, look at those clouds. Don't you love how they spread out in tiers, all of their bottoms a straight line?"

There was no response. Suzanne tried again. "I've taken the week off. Do you want to go to a movie one night?"

"No," she said.

"All right. Is there anything I can do for you since I have some extra time? Anything you'd like me to cook?"

"No."

"I've been thinking maybe we should start eating at the dining room table again and try to get back to some normal things."

"No," she answered, a sharp, definitive answer. Suzann's shoulders relaxed. It was painful to imagine sitting there with two seats empty.

"How are we going to live?" she asked Julie. "It's you and me now. Can you think of some ways we can make a happy home life even if it's different?"

"No."

An hour later they stopped for gas in Newton and switched drivers. Suzanne leaned against the window and closed her eyes until Julie spoke.

"Mom, I want to find Dad. I need to know what's going on with him. Until I figure out what's happened, I can't think about anything else. I told my counsellor that, and she keeps asking what I want to do about finding him and what difference I think it would make. I don't know. I don't know. But I have to do something. Do you think we could hire a private detective?"

"I don't know, Julie. I hadn't thought of that. But it's bothering me, too. Every avenue I've tried gets me nowhere. I even called that woman, Ellen, the one who used to work in the church office, the one he ran away to Colorado with. She said he took off one morning and left her stranded in Denver. She hasn't heard anything since."

"Mother! I can't believe you called her. What did you say?"

"I told her I was trying to find Bell and wondered if she had any idea where he was."

"Did she apologize?"

"No, she didn't even sound guilty. She had no idea where he was, but she said he talked a lot about his parents dying, and about playing football. It sounds to me like he was trying to piece his life together in his own mind.

"Anyway, I tried to find anyone who might be in touch with him—no one in the church office has a clue, and Sadie is trying to find out through the Board of Pensions. But I hadn't thought of a private investigator.

"I agree with you. It's important for us to talk to him to figure out what happened. Dr. Bill says living with ambiguity is especially difficult in a situation like this. Not knowing what has caused your life to suddenly crash leaves you emotionally dizzy, and it's difficult to get your bearings."

Julie shrugged her shoulders. "That sounds true. I feel like I fell down a rabbit hole—like Alice—and nothing is the way it should be. I thought maybe I could mentally put all this in a shoebox on my closet shelf next to the box with my bride and groom dolls and high school keepsakes. I know he'll never really be gone in my memories, but I could leave them on the shelf and get them out when I want to. Then I could go on. I've tried to do that—put this whole thing with dad in the shoebox, but it's like the lid won't stay on, and it keeps falling off the shelf, bothering me."

* * *

At the gate to the festival, a long-haired young man in a cowboy hat clipped pink wristbands on them, gave them programs, and directed them to the parking area on a grassy field. They took their place along with what looked like hundreds of cars.

They walked over beaten-down grass, weaving through the cars toward the entrance, carrying their lawn chairs. Suzanne took a deep breath of country air. The sun warmed her skin, and a gentle breeze cooled it. A faint guitar beat rose and fell with the wind. Finally, on the festival grounds, they consulted their maps. Four stages were listed. Unsure of where to start, they bought some lemonade and sat down at a picnic table to plan their strategy. "We want to see Loretta and her band, for sure," Julie said. "Here, this shows which stage and what time."

Peter had said he'd find them. The Edwards family were also coming, but they weren't sure how early or how many of them could be free that day. Jewell and Ed said they'd be there for sure, and Sarah, too. Matthew was in his first weeks of classes at KU and probably wouldn't join them. Robert wasn't sure he could get away.

"That funnel cake looks good," Julie said, "and the Indian taco, too." She watched a man walking along, balancing both as a small boy held onto his pants leg. A woman with a long braid down her back pulled a red wagon with a toddler resting inside on a bright quilt. A little girl, sporting bows all over her hair, danced in the dirt path. Men and women carried instrument cases or had them slung on their backs: guitars, mandolins, banjos, dulcimers. Most wore cowboy hats, but there were also straw hats, colorful scarfs, and baseball caps from various teams. One woman walked barefoot. She wore a bikini top and denim pants. Many tee shirts proclaimed a message or supported a cause. The most interesting character was an elderly woman, propelling herself around in an electric wheelchair wearing a visor that said "Van Halen Rocks."

Julie squealed when Matthew sneaked up behind her and gave her a big hug. "I didn't think you were coming!"

Jewell and Ed sauntered down the dusty path with Sarah and Robert behind them. Peter jogged up from behind to join them. Julie and Suzanne jumped up to exchange hugs all around; Suzanne held onto Peter as long as she dared.

"Come on," Peter said, "bring your chairs, and I'll show you around. I came yesterday and scoped it out." He showed them Stage IV, a metal building filled with people watching a guitar contest. They stood at the back while two contestants flat-picked their intricate tunes. Then Peter led them to Stage III, an outside area packed with people sitting on folding chairs and blankets. "That's John McCutcheon," he whispered. "You'll love him. Let's stand over here and listen for a while."

The young man with a receding hairline played his guitar with great energy, and the children sang along, "We're a family and we're a tree. Our roots go deep down in history." A young and agile woman beside him put her whole body into signing the song. Some of the children sang and signed along with her. They cheered wildly for the next song, "Rubber Blubber Whale." Suzanne watched the man in front of her holding a young boy on his shoulders and trying to get him to stop pulling his hair.

Peter moved them along, whispering that they could come back later. He took them past the craft barn to a hillside where people sat on the grass. "This is Bluestem—cowboy music," he whispered, and they all sat down. It took Suzanne back to Roy Rogers and Sons of the Pioneers when they sang, "Tumbling Tumbleweeds" and then "When it's Twilight on the Trail."

Loretta's band took the stage after them and sang some good old gospel songs. The crowd loved it and sang along on the choruses. Jewell even knew some Suzanne didn't. She sang along with the crowd, "I'm kind of lonesome for a country where I've never been before." Later she said, "Loretta reminds me of Dolly

Parton."

Next Peter led them to a grandstand. "This is the main stage. You'll want a good seat for the evening performances. You can go up in the stands and be under cover from the sun during the day, but my chair is already set up down between the front seats and the stage for later. I sat there last night, and it was nice under the stars."

They split up leaving all the chairs there in the grandstand with Robert and his dad who wanted to hear an Irish band that was taking the stage next.

"You have all these chairs to keep track of," Jewell said. "Shall I bring you some lunch at noon, a salad, a sandwich?"

"No, Mom," Robert said. "Don't worry about us. You're always feeding us. Take the day off." He winked at her.

She laughed. "I know you two, you're planning a junk food feast. But I guess one day of it won't hurt any of us."

She and Suzanne wandered through the craft booths looking at pottery, jewelry, woodcarvers, luthiers at work, and more. Suzanne spotted Dave and Eileen with baby J. "Jewell, come meet some friends of mine. Friends from church meet friends from another church." Eileen's eyes sparkled as she showed off the sweet baby. Dave smiled broadly.

The next booth held vibrant-colored embroidery pieces whose tiny stitches looked as neat on the back as on the front. A petite woman with brown button eyes and a heavily wrinkled face welcomed them. Behind her a mural showed the Mekong River running through China, Vietnam, Laos, Thailand, and Cambodia.

Suzanne and Jewell examined the scarves and framed pictures while another woman engaged the seller in conversation. "Are you from Vietnam?"

"Yes, and Thailand," the seamstress said.

"Did you come here because of the war?"

"Yes, my husband killed. I go Thailand, come US."

"I'm sorry to hear that. My nephew was killed as well."

The women clasped hands.

Later, Suzanne and Jewell joined Ed, Peter, and Sarah in the flat area between the main stage and the stands as Peter had recommended. In between acts they told each other what they had seen and heard. Beppe Gambetta was Sarah's favorite. Peter liked Tom Chapin and also the Dixie Chicks. Ed agreed with him. "They are going places, mark my words."

Eventually, Julie and Matthew walked toward them slowly, holding hands, hardly acknowledging anyone else as they took their seats.

Daylight faded, the breeze cooled, and the main acts began. During John McCutcheon's song "Christmas in the Trenches," about a WWI spontaneous Christmas truce, Suzanne looked around at her children, their best friends and her best friends and all the other shining faces celebrating peace. Babies slept between their parents on blankets on the ground. Off to one side, youngsters twirled and whirled around in the dark, and pre-teen girls danced in the light near the stage. The moon and stars grew brighter. Geese flew overhead honking. A train whistled by.

John sang "Joe Hill," about a labor activist and "Happy Adoption Day." Then to cheers, he sang "Calling all the Children Home." It started with his mother calling all of her children home for dinner and ended with a world-wide call for all the children to come to the table. I'll work that into a sermon on World Communion Sunday, Suzanne thought. When he ended his set with "Alleluia, The Great Storm is Over," people stood and raised their arms for the chorus, "Lift up your wings and fly."

Suzanne let tears dry on her face. I'll never ever miss this, she told herself. I'll be here every year. These are my people.

Chapter 20

They left the festival at eleven, full of music. On the drive home, Julie burst into song several times. "Alleluia, the great storm is over. Lift up your wings and fly." Suzanne drank coffee to stay awake. The next day started her vacation week, so she didn't have to get up early.

Julie fell asleep for a while but then woke up and chattered all the way home. "Matthew likes KU, and he wants to show me which dorm he thinks I'd like. I'm so glad we'll be there together. I didn't know if he would change a lot when he went to college. I thought he might outgrow me.

"Mom, did you ever think you and Dad might get divorced? I mean like when you first dated, when we were little, any time?"

"No, I never did. It never entered my mind. Other people divorced, and I lived through their pain with them, but I was sure it would never happen to us. So sure. Now sometimes I wonder why I thought I was above all that."

"Did you think Dad was unhappy?"

"No. He never said he wanted anything to be different. I thought he was rather settled, maybe too settled, in his routine."

"Could it be God's will that he leave and start a new life?"

"I doubt it. Not everything that happens is God's will. When someone goes against God's ways, they suffer the consequences."

"And hurt other people, too."

"Yes."

"But we always said God can make good come from even the worst things. Even this?"

There's no way, she thought, but she said, "I guess so."

"Mom, I'm still thinking about getting a P.I. to help find him. But I know we don't have the money for that, so I'm praying we'll find another way. I really need to talk to him."

"I know you do, sweetheart. I know."

* * *

The week off for Suzanne coincided with fall weather settling over her neighborhood. She took Wolfie on walks morning and afternoon, up the hill, past the golf course to streets where the houses looked like mansions, and ancient trees towered over them, unusually big trees for Kansas. The oaks and sugar maples were still mostly green, but they held hints around the edges of the colors to come. Some leaves had already begun dropping. They crunched underfoot. Acorns begged to be kicked. The crisp air in the morning invigorated her and the afternoon sun hugged her with warmth. But when the sun set, the dark and biting grief washed over her again.

One afternoon Julie walked with her. "Mom, all my friends graduated with Peter. I never realized this was going to happen. It's my senior year, and it's not any fun. I want to get out of there."

"I remember that feeling. We called it 'senioritis,' and one of my friends ruined her grade average by mentally checking out."

"I won't do that, but these days drag on and on."

"What are you looking forward to?"

"First, the weekend. Let's go to a movie or shopping or something."

"Sounds like fun."

"Then Sunday it's my turn to take care of the nursery kids. I love playing with them. Let's see. What else am I looking forward to? Thanksgiving. Peter will be home, and we'll have lots of fun. But that's going to be weird without Dad." She kicked an acorn down the sidewalk.

"I'm trying to decide what I want to do with my life. For a while I was sure I wanted to be a kindergarten teacher, but lately I've been wondering about social work or being a pastor."

"A pastor? You've never mentioned that before."

"Peter was always going to do that, but he hasn't talked about it lately. I didn't want to look like I was copying him. Do you think I'd be good at it?"

"Absolutely. You are loving, caring, and compassionate. You have a heart for God and a good measure of wisdom."

"But what about the preaching and dealing with people's problems. I don't know how to do those things."

"You learn a lot in college and seminary, and then you learn from doing it. You already know the Bible well, but you will learn more about how it all fits together, and you'll be able to see more clearly God's revelation to us over the centuries. Mostly, I learned how to think and how to search for truth. You also learn how to be a leader who stands up for justice especially for those who have no power. And you learn to share power with people rather than holding power over them."

"How do you know what to say to people? I've seen you pray just the right thing. Like last Sunday when we visited Mrs. Barker at the nursing home. There she was with Alzheimer's, and I didn't know what to say, but you talked to her and even made her smile, and your prayer was beautiful. How do you do that?"

"I pray before I go in that God will use me to help. I consider what the person might be feeling and what they might need. If they can talk to me, I listen carefully for clues and follow up on their concerns. One skill I'm always working on is asking the right question at the right time. It's so much better than going in with a set patter and a few Bible verses that don't fit where the person is."

"I don't know how you can take care of so many people. And they all have different, hard situations. I only know some of them; I assume they tell you other things that I don't know about."

Suzanne nodded. "As I look back, I can see how my love of people has deepened and broadened over the years. It's not easy to like some people, but loving them is a gift from God. What I like about being a pastor is being with people in their difficulties and their happy times and holding before us what I know of the hope and abundant joy God offers. You know, it's Jesus' way of life.

"I am involved with more crises and joys than most people are in a lifetime because I'm like a member of the family for so many people. I gladly stand with them and gather the community to stand with them, too."

"It's like you're a stand-in for Jesus."

"I never thought about it that way."

"I'm going to think some more about being a pastor, but don't tell anybody. I haven't mentioned it to Matthew; I'm not sure what he'll think of the idea."

* * *

When Peter called on Sunday afternoon, Julie mentioned the private investigator idea as Suzanne picked up the extension.

"Let's do it," he said.

"But we don't know how much it would cost," Julie said before Suzanne could.

"Yeah, we probably couldn't afford it. But maybe we could approach the problem like a P.I. would. First, he—."

"Or she," Julie interjected.

"Or she would trace Dad's last steps, at least what we know about that. And then she or he would call everybody who knows him to see if they've heard from him."

"I think we've done that ... sorta," Julie said. "You know, Mom asked 'that woman' he went to Colorado with. She didn't know anything. She said he took off without telling her."

"Mom, you called her?" Peter said. "Nobody ever tells me anything. I can't believe you did that. What else did she say?"

Julie broke in, "Mom, didn't she tell you he'd been talking about the past a lot?"

"Yes, she did say that he talked about his parents dying right after he started college."

"Did he have any friends he might go see in Pennsylvania or from his days in Ohio?" Peter asked.

"Mom?" Julie prompted.

"I'm thinking. In Ohio he didn't have any close friends except Frances and Chet. In Pennsylvania his family is all gone. The last cousin died some time ago."

"What about college?" Julie asked. "Didn't that woman say he was talking about college?"

"There was a coach he always quoted," Peter said. "'Follow through on everything.' Remember that? Do you know who that was?"

"Coach PT," Suzanne said. "Petey. His first name was Peter. I think that's why your dad wanted to name you Peter, though he never said so."

"Is he still coaching? Did Dad keep in touch?" Julie asked.

"I don't know, but I'll look back through last year's Christmas cards to find his address. I think there is one from him."

CHAPTER 21

SUZANNE found Coach PT's address, and the reference librarian in his hometown gave her his phone number. She gripped the phone tightly and dialed. "Coach, hello. This is Suzanne Hawkins. You probably don't remember me. I'm married to Bell Hawkins. He played for you in the mid-sixties. I'm calling on the chance that he might have contacted you. We're trying to find him. He left home suddenly, and we—our kids—."

"Yes, yes, Suzanne. I remember. I was at your wedding. Bell was here last week, and we had a good visit."

"He was? Do you know where he is?"

"I think so. He wasn't himself. We had a long, long talk, and he stayed here for a few days. Then I connected him with my daughter, who is a nurse at a local rehab facility. She got him into a program. He wasn't supposed to have visitors at first so I haven't seen him. I don't know how he's doing."

"Thank God. We've been so worried about him. He didn't say why he was leaving. We need to talk with him, especially our daughter Julie, who is a senior in high school, and our son Peter, who is a freshman in college. It's difficult for all of us. We don't know what he's going through. Do you think if we showed up at the rehab facility, we could talk with him?"

"I don't know, Suzanne, and I don't have their phone number, but I'll call my daughter and see what I can find out. I'll call you back as soon as I have any information."

He called a few hours later as she and Julie were eating dinner and watching Jeopardy. "My daughter said they couldn't guarantee he'd see you on any certain day, but she said it might work out. Let me give you directions to my house. It's easy to find. You can come here, and I'll take you over there."

Julie and Peter wanted to go even if they might not get to see him. And they wanted to go alone. Suzanne balked. "Why? I need to talk with him, too," she said.

"Mom, we need to do this," Julie said. "Besides, he might talk to us if you're not there. Sarah and Matthew are asking their parents if they can go with us. Please, let us do this. We're not children any more. We want to do this on our own."

Suzanne called Jewell. "What do you think about our kids taking a trip by themselves?"

"At first I said no, but then they kept telling me how they had planned it out. Last night Robert said he'd go with them if it would help. I will feel more relaxed if he goes. And they are all good drivers."

"That does sound better," Suzanne said. "Robert has such a level head—well, they all do, but he's older. Still, I can't believe we'd let them drive cross country. I really want to go, but I'm so angry with Bell maybe they will do better without me. They need to talk to their dad. They need to know he cares about them. I'll worry about them, but how can I deny them this chance? I'll think about it a little longer, but if Robert goes, I'm more inclined to say yes."

Suzanne examined their map and their estimated timetable. She asked them what they would do if they had a flat tire, if they ran out of gas, if they got lost. They answered reasonably. Smart kids, she thought. I had no idea they knew how to handle such emergencies.

Finally, she told them they could go. But then her dreams rumbled and tumbled. In one, they ran out of gas in the middle of the night in a dark wooded area. In another, they drove off a cliff. She woke up exhausted every morning.

On the Tuesday before Thanksgiving, Peter, Julie and Suzanne stayed all night with the Edwards in Middletown. The four young people got up to a chilly dawn, threw pillows into the back of Robert's Yukon, accepted hot chocolate from Jewell and a cooler of food from Suzanne, and drove off. Jewell, Ed, and Suzanne stood at the door waving until the car turned the corner, and then they rushed inside to warm themselves with coffee by the fireplace.

"At least the weather is supposed to be good," Ed said.

"God be with them," Suzanne said. "We should have prayed before they left."

"God, grant them wisdom and quick reflexes and a good, successful trip," Jewell added. "Here's a copy of their final itinerary, which Sarah typed up for each of us. It's a lot to cover, but they've figured it out. If everything goes according to plan, they could be back in time to have Saturday and Sunday to rest up before school starts again on Monday. If their plans change, they'll have two days' flexibility."

"I'm glad they're staying with Frances and Chet going and coming back," Suzanne said. "They may need some wise counsel. No telling what Bell will do."

Julie called Wednesday night from Frances and Chet's house in Columbus. "We did great on the trip, Mom. It was lots of fun, and we saw the arch in St. Louis. We bought a hat for Robert; it looks like a chauffeur's cap. We act like he's our driver and we're wealthy brats. Tomorrow we'll leave early in the morning so we can be in Pittsburgh by about lunch time. We'll have a nice long visit with Dad. Then we'll come back to Columbus for Thanksgiving dinner with Frances and Chet tomorrow evening."

Suzanne breathed a sigh of relief. *Thank you, God, that they are safe and in good spirits. Please move Bell's heart and soften it so they may have some resolution to their questions. Give me your wisdom to help them deal with this trauma. O God, I pray they will come out of it stronger. And help me remember your many gifts as I celebrate Thanksgiving Day.*

That was easier said than done. Jewell and Ed had offered to cancel their plans to go to his aunt's in Kansas City so they could spend Thanksgiving Day with Suzanne, but she wouldn't hear of it. She also had turned down invitations from Loretta and Eileen. She didn't want to cast a shadow on anybody else's day.

Thursday morning Suzanne awakened to the sound of rain on the roof. Alternating heavy and light showers played a rhythm all their own. She sank deeper into her pillow and deeper inside herself.

She had planned to keep the holiday traditions, cooking a big meal and having it ready to reheat when the kids came back home. Maybe I'll go ahead and start playing Christmas music, she thought. I could even get out the decorations and have the house full of joy when they come back. But it all seemed so lame, an artificial attempt to jump start her heart. However, since the turkey was thawed, she removed the giblets, shoved it in the oven, and went back to bed. Wolfie padded up the stairs behind her. She picked him up, and he snuggled in close to her.

* * *

The phone rang, waking her to a dark room and the drumming of heavy rain. Disoriented, she answered and somehow managed not to give away her grogginess. "Suzanne, Happy Thanksgiving," Frances said. "They're back safe and sound, and my but they are fine young people. Here's Julie."

"Mom, he left the rehab place. He's living in an apartment near there and working at a bar. We had to go to the bar to see him." She choked up and Peter took the phone.

"He didn't look happy to see us. His eyes looked funny, like he wasn't focusing. All he would say is, 'I needed to start over and get a new life.' I kept my cool for a while, but I was feeling a blood rush. So, I said to him, 'Are you abandoning me as your son and Julie as your daughter? Don't we count anymore?' He kept looking down at the bar while we sat across from him. He never even touched us, no hand shake, no hug, no nothing. He never looked up. We waited a long time for him to say something. When he didn't, Julie said, 'I want my dad back.' She started crying and everybody was looking at us. Then I got mad. I wanted to shake him and wake him up. I guess I caused a scene, yelling at him and using words I won't tell you."

Julie took the phone. "Can you believe Dad would do that? He's not the same person. Peter and I agreed—he's like a stranger. Mom, you wouldn't know him. I asked him if he would write to me. He shook his head." She choked and coughed. "All he would say was, 'I need to start over.' Peter said, 'You can't throw your children out like trash,' but Dad kept shaking his head. I was crying all through this, and a man came over—I think he was the owner—and asked Dad to sit down at a table and talk with us, but Dad shook his head."

Julie was crying, and Peter came back on the phone. "I asked him what we'd done to deserve this. That's the only time he looked up. He said, 'Nothing. Nothing.' So then I asked him why—why did he run away? And from then on he looked at the bar and wouldn't say any more."

"Peter, I'm so sorry it turned out like this. I thought—I don't know what I thought he'd do, but not this. He's certainly not himself."

Julie came back on the phone. "Mom, Coach PT was real nice. He told us what a good football player Dad was and how hard it was on him when his parents both died his freshman year. Coach showed us the rehab place and then helped find where Dad was working. He waited for us outside the bar with Matthew, Sarah and Robert, and then when we were ready, he gave us directions to get back to Columbus. We thanked him a lot. He said he'd call you if he heard anything new. I think he was sad, too."

"I'm sorry it didn't turn out like you'd hoped, Julie. I don't understand this at all. You are very brave to go try."

Peter was back. "Mom, we have to figure out how to go on without him. We can't make him love us. Julie asked him where the cats were. I still can't believe he took the cats and didn't even leave any word for us. Julie was still hoping we could bring them home. We think he probably took them to a rescue place. We don't know if they're …." His voice cracked.

Frances took the phone. "Suzanne, we've talked some and I'll be here for them if they want to talk more. They're still planning to leave for home early in the morning. I'll call if there's any change in that. But how are you? How did you spend Thanksgiving Day?"

"I'm fine. I cooked a turkey."

"Hang in there. You're a strong woman. By the way, I'm working on Advent sermons, and I'd like to run some thoughts by you. Are you free for some sermon talk tomorrow?"

"Sure, sure. I've started on an Advent series. Yes, I'll be here."

* * *

The next morning Frances called. "I didn't realize how old I was until I saw those young people act like it was nothing to make that round trip in three days."

"Yes, I know what you mean. They should get to Middletown sometime late tonight. I'll pick my two up, and they'll have Saturday and Sunday to sleep. How are they doing?"

"Amazingly well, given Bell's despicable response or non-response to them. They asked Chet and me lots of questions about what he was like when we first met him. We told them about the good times the four of us had together and our long talks about clergy couples. Remember how we agonized over ways we wouldn't let any church come between us?"

"Yes, I remember. Thanks for letting them stay with you, and double thanks for talking with them."

"You're welcome. We also told them how much their dad loved them and that this behavior isn't anything we'd have expected of him. And we listened for any hint they thought it was their fault, you know the way kids do. I didn't pick that up. By the way, I think having Robert along helped a lot. He sure is a wise young man."

"Good. Good. Now I'm seeing that it was probably better I didn't go. No telling what I'd have done when Bell acted like that. I have visions of punching him in the stomach."

"Yeah, I'd have kicked him where it really hurts!"

"Yes, that's the spirit. I'm glad you're angry for me."

"You know I'm here anytime you want to talk?"

"Thanks, Frances. You're the best." Suzanne willed herself to relax those tightened muscles ready to punch someone. "Do you still want to talk sermons?"

"Sure. What are you doing for Advent?"

"Our theme is light, starting this Sunday with I John 1, 'God is light.' Christmas Eve we'll read John 1, 'The light shines in the darkness, but the darkness has not put it out.' Julie and our friend Loretta are helping me plan worship for Advent. I told you about Loretta, our own Dolly Parton. Julie suggested we give the children little flashlights on Christmas Eve instead of candles. And I'm going to try to get a big searchlight like car dealers use to draw people to them. You know, the kind that circles through the sky? The other Sundays we'll read 'You are the light of the world' and 'Let your light so shine that people may see your good works and praise God,' and maybe 'Whoever follows me will never walk in darkness, but will have the light of life.' That's as far as I am. What are you working on?"

"I'm exploring grace, but I don't know if it will take all Advent, so I'm not calling it a series. I'm wondering though if I might use your dream about the communion wine turning to blood. I think that would be a great illustration of grace."

"How do you figure it was about grace? I don't see it."

"Think about it this way: In the dream you are tired, weary to the bone, looking for some escape. You need refreshing of your spirit and your body."

"Yes, but I don't get either one in the dream."

"You don't get exactly what you think you need, but you do receive the grace of God, a blessing without doing anything to earn it."

"Interesting. It seems to me it's more about sacrifice. But feel free to use it. Send me a copy so I can see what I'm missing."

* * *

The Sunday after Thanksgiving, Peter and Julie surprised Suzanne by going to church with her. Amy's parents had planned to drive her and Peter back to school, but at the last minute Amy called to say she had another ride, and there wasn't room for Peter. So, the three of them went to church and planned to drive to Winfield after lunch. Loretta asked Peter and Julie to sing with her during the worship service. They joined her with harmonies on the chorus:

> *I sing because I'm happy*
> *I sing because I'm free*
> *His eye is on the sparrow*
> *And I know he watches me.*

Suzanne held the words close to her.

* * *

On the way to Winfield, Julie drove and Peter sat next to her. He turned and looked over his shoulder, "Mom, Dad didn't even look like himself. He's lost weight and grown a beard."

"I wonder what will happen to him," Julie said. "I keep trying to think what might save him. It's like everything inside him has disintegrated, and what's left is a shell."

Peter threw his hands up in the air. "I don't know what else we can do. He has to want his life to be different."

"I keep praying for him," Suzanne said. "One day, I think he will contact you both and want to have a relationship. It may take a long time for that to happen, but he's suffering, and I hope you will hold him in a special prayer deep in your hearts until that time comes."

"If it ever does," Peter said. "But it's his choice. And you know what? It's time I made some choices, too. I've had it with Amy. What did I ever see in that selfish, inconsiderate, egomaniac? Talk about a shell."

The anger fell into silence. Good, Suzanne thought. He didn't see that in her the time she threw his class ring at him and not when she broke up right before prom. But this is when he sees it? Whatever it takes. I'm glad he's seen the light.

After a long silence Julie asked, "Have you chosen a major yet?"

"No, I have time."

"Do you still think about being a pastor?"

"Not lately, but my counsellor is awesome. I might think about pastoral counseling."

Chapter 22

THE next week Dr. Bill listened intently as Suzanne described the trip to see Bell and his disappointing response. "It wasn't just disappointing, it was despicable. I want to punch him."

She looked for a response but he simply nodded and waited. "But I don't need to talk about that," she said.

"What do you want to talk about today?"

"I'm not sure. There's so much."

"Last time we talked you were still feeling exhausted. How have you been feeling lately?"

"Still exhausted, so much on my mind, so much I need to do, no energy to do it all."

"Let's make a list of all the things you have on your mind." He looked to her for agreement, and she nodded. "You rattle them off and I'll take notes."

- Peter. I'm concerned that we don't talk more often. With his dad gone, I'm afraid he will become more distant.
- Julie is unhappy, tired of high school. What can I do to help her?
- What effect will Bell's abandonment have on both kids? How can I help them?
- Bell. What part did I have in this?—it's sad, so sad. He's lost his life. Will he survive? What can I do to help him?

- Church. Are we doing enough? We need to have more mission than survival. Is the support of Alcoholics Anonymous groups enough?
- Is there more I can do to connect with the young people?
- How can we be more inviting to the people in the neighborhood?
- Me. Will I survive? What does the future hold? Should I be doing more to get the grief over and go on? Will anyone ever love me and cherish me—I mean a man?
- Am I hurting this church by continuing when I'm not at my best? How can I live alone? Should I move?
- Money. How will I manage with two kids in college?
- Will Dr. Bill give up on me?

She ended with a grin.

"That's quite a list," he said looking deep into her eyes in that way he had of revealing his own soul and loving hers. Don't even think about his sexy blue eyes, she reminded herself. "Have you ever been called an overachiever?" he asked.

"Yes, several times. My granddad said, 'You go after everything like killing a snake.'"

He nodded. "By the way, I will never give up on you, and I hope you will never give up on yourself. You are doing well.

"This list gives me a better picture of the burdens you walk around with and why in your dreams you are often lying on the ground, unable to walk and having to pull yourself along.

"Now, tell me the dream again." This was the third time he'd asked her to recount it.

She smiled. "Have you forgotten it, or are you seeing if I change the way I tell it?"

He laughed and his bright blue eyes crinkled. "I haven't forgotten it. But I do want to see if it has grown in your mind or shifted into a clearer meaning."

She told him the dream again. "It seems like a significant dream, but I don't get it," Suzanne said. "It still sounds as if I feel weary and try to get away to relax, but there is no escape from people needing me. In the dream I feel guilty for resenting them, and so I give in and let them touch me. They're healed, and I'm happy for them. Sounds rather selfish or grandiose, doesn't it?"

"Not really. The tone would be different, I think. You probably would want to be the center of attention and power. Tell me, what is your prayer when you are weary?"

"It's usually to be given more energy and wisdom in order to help people."

"And yet, in the dream you weren't looking for more energy and wisdom to help others. You were looking for some respite from that."

"Yes, I wanted rest, but then the wine spilled, it turned to blood, and people were healed. It sounds like someone else's dream, not mine."

"But in your prayers you usually ask for more ability to help others?"

"Yes."

"And your list is full of wanting to have more energy to help the people in your life. Do you ever pray for them to be helped without your involvement?"

She closed her eyes and thought back. "No, I don't think so."

"Why do you think that is?"

"Seems to me when I pray for someone, I ought to be willing to stand by them and do what I can for them."

"Physically or spiritually?"

"Both but more spiritually or emotionally. That's what I have to offer."

"And what kind of healing did Jesus do?"

She thought. "It was physical, but then he'd often say, 'Your sins are forgiven' so I guess it was both."

"I'm thinking out loud, Suzanne, following a rabbit trail. Are you okay to go this direction?"

"Yes, sure. I'm with you, I think. I don't heal people physically, yet the dream was about physical healing that came through me without me doing anything. I hope this isn't a call for me to be a faith healer."

"Why is that?"

"I don't know. I said that quickly, without thinking. I guess it is the connotation, the shyster factor, the demands it would make."

"Have you ever prayed for a physical healing?"

"I prayed for Peter when he had a head injury. I prayed a lot."

"How do you feel right now?" he asked.

"Confused. My thoughts are jumbled. I think some journaling will help. It's all connected somehow: the dream, communion bread and wine, body and blood, the spiritual and physical, my prayers. Remember the questions Frances suggested a while back? Maybe it's time to look at those again. I can't remember what they were, but I have them written down here in my journal." She shuffled through the pages. "That was back shortly after—here it is."

> *Are you doing what God has called you to do, or are you trying to do God's work, too?*
>
> *You ask God to give you strength to do what's needed. Have you considered any other prayer?*

"This is all coming together but I can't quite see it yet," she said.

"What are the answers to her questions?"

"Trying to do God's work? Yes, using everything I have. I guess if I see a need, I move toward it. I think I can make a difference, and I often do."

"Where do you end? Where does God begin?" Dr. Bill asked.

"I don't know. Maybe at the end of my ability … the end of

my energy? Frances says I should let Jesus do some of the work, but I don't know how to do that, I don't know what it means."

"So you overwork?"

"I don't know how not to. There are always important matters left on my list at the end of a week. I always feel guilty."

"Why do you work yourself to exhaustion?" he asked.

"I don't know. It could be to be successful. It could be to make sure everything comes out all right for everybody. All my life, my wish blowing out birthday candles has been 'that we all be happy.' I also like to keep everything orderly and organized. Bell said that was controlling, but I don't think so. I do what I can to make sure all will go well. But here I am. None of that is working. My life is out of control." She looked out the window at a light snow beginning to cover the branches of a dogwood tree. "That sounds like the first of the twelve steps of AA," she muttered.

After a long pause, Dr. Bill asked, "Do you remember the words?"

"Yes, I've heard them often in my congregation. 'We admitted we were powerless over alcohol—that our lives had become unmanageable. Came to believe that a Power greater than ourselves could restore us to sanity. Made a decision to turn our will and our lives over to the care of God as we understood Him.'"

"They have taught you well. Are you at the place where you need to say this for yourself?"

"I never thought of it that way. I guess I thought everything depended on me. I'm not sure where my faith has been concerning the dailyness of duties except believing God would give me strength to do everything."

"In your dream you aren't making anything happen. You are in fact out of control, exhausted from trying to do too much."

"Yes, that's right, then the wine is spilled on me, it turns to blood, and people are healed. I stand there and let it happen."

"How is that different from the way you typically live your

life?"

"In the dream, Jesus worked through me without me planning it."

"Write that down," he said.

She did and then looked up at him. "I don't have to work so hard?"

He smiled.

"I don't know if I can keep a job without working to my limits."

"What is the alternative?"

"Let's see. Frances would say to let Jesus do some of the work."

"What does your dream tell you?"

"That healing can come without my making it happen. And Frances's questions fit right in. My prayer doesn't always have to be, 'Help me do this.' Sometimes it needs to be—or all the time it needs to be, 'How can I help you, God? What is your will? What do you want me to do?'

"So, my life has become unmanageable." She looked up at the ceiling and closed her eyes. "A Power greater than myself can restore me to sanity. I need to turn my will and my life over to the care of God."

She repeated the words in her mind. *A Power greater than myself can restore me to sanity. I will turn my will and my life over to the care of God in a way I haven't done before.*

After a long silence, she looked at Dr. Bill. His eyes were closed. When he finally opened them, she said, "I thought I had done that, but now I see I've not been acting with as much faith and trust as I thought I had."

Dr. Bill looked at her with a big grin on his face. "That's beautiful," he said.

She started to smile but then her eyes floated up. "Wait, I think the questions I had about the blood, the wine, and communion fit in here …. Nope. Lost it."

"You're tired. That's a whale of a lot of work for one day. Go home, rest, write in your journal. Let it settle down. We'll start here next time."

* * *

The Christmas season picked up speed. Suzanne decided they would have a traditional holiday at home. No moping around. She decorated with energy born from anger and determination. Julie helped her pick out a live tree—Bell never liked the mess of one. And they decorated with every ornament they had—another thing Bell never liked. He always wanted a perfectly shaped artificial tree and none of the handmade ornaments. She and Julie baked Mexican wedding cakes and decorated sugar cookies. Buying gifts was more difficult. She'd never done that without Bell, and without him there was no rhythm. She had always made notes of ideas for each one on their list, and they'd go shopping for hours until they finally agreed on the perfect gifts. Now, any time she shopped, she felt alone and lonely, as though the prickles of her grief could be seen by every person she passed. She looked with new eyes at men shopping alone, wondering if any of them felt like she did.

At church the wreaths on the front doors, the Christmas tree in the sanctuary, and candles in the windows raised her spirits. Julie was with her every Sunday, and after dinner at Loretta's, they'd go shopping or visiting in the hospital or nursing homes. Sometimes Loretta joined them, generating laughter and singing.

"Suzanne, that series of sermons about light is hitting the mark with some of our AA folks," she said. "One man told me, 'I've seen that light the pastor talked about, and it blinded me like it did Paul. Then I got up and changed my ways.'"

"God is good," Suzanne said.

"Did you ever find a big searchlight for Christmas Eve?"

"I've called three car dealers. None of them have their own light. They rent one when they need it, and it's quite pricey. I'm still hoping I can make it happen." She heard herself say, "I can." Maybe God can take this one, she thought. No, that's not right. Stop telling God what to do. God, what would you have me do?

The lessons were slow in coming, but occasionally, even in the busy season, she noticed when she tried to carry everything on her back. But she hadn't done any of the decoration planning at church. May and her friends made all the decisions, and then others assisted. Suzanne enjoyed helping some of the little children decorate the tree with symbols of the faith. She put ornaments high where they pointed but couldn't reach, and they placed many on the bottom, clapping and squealing. Eileen helped J place a fish on a limb. J patted it and made it swing. One woman approached Suzanne. "I can come back later and even out the tree decorations." But Suzanne wouldn't let anything the children did be moved.

The week before Christmas, she still hadn't found a searchlight, and decided to give up. "It was such a good idea," she said to Loretta. "I hoped someone might follow the light and come for Christmas Eve service."

One evening at dusk as she headed home, she encountered a detour and had to wind around back roads to get far enough north to enter the interstate. She drove through Chisholm, past the drug store and the mortuary, smiling at the glimpse of the old west. Then she made a u turn and went back the way she had come. The Bordello Club. Was that a searchlight out front? Yes. It sat on the corner but wasn't shining. Three cars sat in the parking lot. Lights on the roof outlined the dancing girls. Do I dare go in there? What if someone sees me? Double dog dare you, she said to herself.

She took a deep breath, looked around warily, and got out of the car. Hitching her purse up on her shoulder, she strode to the dark entrance. She pulled open the heavy door. Her eyes gradually adjusted to the dim, smoky light. A bar ran along the wall to her left. A small stage on the wall furthest from the door sat empty. The smell of overripe fruit tickled her nose. Beer, she thought. No one was in sight, but she heard people talking from a room behind the bar.

She walked toward it. "Hello?"

A red-headed young man appeared, wiping his hands on a towel. "Can I help you?"

"I, uh, I'm, well, that is, I'm wondering if I could borrow your searchlight for a few hours on Christmas Eve."

He looked at her like she had two heads, and she could see him start to shake his head so she went on quickly. "I'm the pastor of Lamb of God Presbyterian Church, down the road, and I have my heart set on having a searchlight shining around the sky to welcome people to our Christmas Eve service. The children will have small flashlights, and they'll sing, 'This Little Light of Mine'. And I could ...." She stopped herself before offering to put a thank you to them in the bulletin.

He scratched his head and shook it. "Let me get the owner. You can ask him. You want something to drink while you wait?"

"Diet Coke?" she asked. He quickly complied without the smirk she expected, and he refused her money. She waited patiently, giggling quietly as she thought about telling Loretta what she'd done.

The owner came around and sat on the bar stool next to her. She tensed. From the waist up he looked like a lawyer with his round glasses, white shirt, tie and jacket. From the waist down he looked like a cowboy in skin tight jeans and cowboy boots. "Tell me what you want with the searchlight," he said.

She told him about the church, the sermon, the idea of a light sweeping the sky on Christmas Eve. "The car dealers all rent theirs and it's too expensive for us to do that."

He stared at her and chewed his lip. "How long you been at that church?"

"Since May."

"When I was a child I went to Christmas Eve services at a Methodist Church close to there. Do you have little candles?"

"Yes, everybody has a candle to light."

They were interrupted by three young women coming in the door. "Rev. Suzanne, these here are our dancers, Peggy and Juliet and Bebe. Girls, this here pastor wants to use our searchlight on Christmas Eve. Do you think we can trust her?"

"Why, sure, Mac. Let her use it," Peggy said.

"Where's the church?" Juliet asked.

Bebe squinted at her. "Are you one of those crusaders looking to get us in trouble?"

"No, no crusade here. But you'd all be welcome to come to the service. The church is on the corner of North Arkansas and 48th. I have this crazy idea about a searchlight. I've been preaching about light. You know, Jesus is the light of the world. The wise men followed a star. We're giving the children flashlights and they're going to sing, 'This Little Light of Mine.'"

"Aww, that sounds sweet," Peggy said.

Not only did Mac let her borrow the light. He hauled it in his truck, set it up, and stayed around to watch over it.

As people arrived, many stood outside in the frigid air and watched the searchlight shine around the sky. The children pointed up following its path.

The sanctuary filled up with people, many Suzanne didn't recognize. Loretta covered her mouth to stifle her laughter when Suzanne told her how she found the searchlight. Later, she confirmed that a dancer she knew, Juliet, came in at the last minute. She thought maybe the other two Suzanne described were there, too.

Suzanne saw Dave talking with Mac in the back of the sanctuary shortly before the service started. Then during the candle lighting she saw him take a candle out to the back and hand it to him. Now, that's evangelism, she thought. Dave is an evangelist in his bones, and I don't think he even knows it.

Early in the service, Julie and Peter gathered the children to sit on the steps in front of the pulpit. They handed each one a small flashlight and turned it on for them. Immediately miniature searchlights shone on the walls and ceilings and pews. When they regained the children's attention, Julie and Suzanne sat with the children to sing, and Peter faced them mouthing the words to "This Little Light of Mine." Carl's daughter Ella and three of her friends sang beautifully while younger ones were too busy shining their lights to sing about it. Eileen sat at the edge of the group of children holding J on her lap. Now ten months old, J stared at the children singing and clapped along with the song. The children singing was the highlight of the evening for Suzanne, although Loretta's "Joy to the World" was beautiful, too. At the end of the service, Suzanne lit the candles held by those on the aisle, and they passed the light one to the other as they all sang "Silent Night." The room glowed with candlelight and faces shone bright with joy.

* * *

On Christmas Day, Suzanne, Peter, and Julie moved around each other in the kitchen preparing a feast and singing along with their favorite Christmas records. Julie presented a golden brown Cornish hen on rice for each of them. Peter made a red and green gelatin salad with a cream cheese layer like his grandmother always did. Suzanne made rolls like her grandmother used to. Their sweet yeasty smell brought back many memories for her.

They sat at the dining room table for the first time since Bell had left. Julie had turned it around and shoved one side against the wall. She put a poinsettia on that end so there was no empty chair at the table.

Julie prayed, "God, we celebrate your birth as Jesus, and we are thankful for all that he taught us and showed us about who you are. We don't know where Dad is today, but we hope he is safe and that he is healthier and that he comes back to us someday."

Chapter 23

THE new year began with record-setting cold weather which kept people inside whenever possible. One Sunday they had to call off church when the furnace failed and couldn't be repaired soon enough.

Suzanne put her house and the church back in order, holiday decorations along with holiday cheer packed away. She kept busy, but tinges of depression floated close behind her and occasionally caught up.

Discussions with Dr. Bill helped some. "You nourish many people, you take care of so much. What nourishes you? Who takes care of you?"

She closed her eyes. "My sisters and I visit on the phone, but we're all so busy it's not like it used to be. I'd like to be closer to them. Peter calls on Sunday afternoons. Julie and I have time together. Frances, as you know, is a caring friend."

"Do you go to movies, read books, do crafts of some kind?"

"I used to. There seems to be no time lately."

"Remember Frances's sermon on grace?" he asked.

"Yes, the one that included my dream and the scripture, 'My yoke is easy, and my burden is light.' Maybe I should get a yoke and put it up in my office to remind me that burdens which are mine to bear ride easily on my shoulders."

"You could get one for home, too." He grinned, and she reminded herself once again that this charming, generous, wise man was not available for more than a professional relationship.

"Maybe I should put pictures of yokes everywhere so I'll see them regularly. 'Come to me, all you that are weary and are carrying heavy burdens and I will give you rest.' That's an amazing gift. With all the holiday fuss, I haven't kept it in mind as much as I wanted to. But now is the time to accept that."

"If you're like me," he said. "You'll find yourself learning the same lessons over and over."

"Yes, I can see that. I try to remember that feeling the first time it came clear to me that I don't have the burden of doing everything for everybody—and there is no way for me to control life. My shoulders felt lighter—even physically. They actually rose up in the air they were so light. At times I remember that and feel great freedom from all the *oughts* and *shoulds*."

"Freedom," he repeated and paused.

"Yes, I've been journaling about that. It's physical and spiritual and emotional. Like my dream: I didn't see the physical wine/blood as healing. It felt as if it were simply out of my control. Now, I'm thinking it represents freedom from having to be in control of everything. This is a major, life-changing learning. I suppose it will take me a long, long time to accept this gift fully."

Dr. Bill nodded. "Maybe your shoulders will remind you."

They talked about the empty nest coming. "We've talked over these past months about who you are at your core without all your titles. You've done some good journaling. And I think rereading that regularly will help you set your sight on next steps in your life.

"When Julie leaves, it will be another opportunity to exercise your strength and get clearer about who you are. It would be good to think about what you've always wanted to do but never had the time for."

"I know what it is. I've always wanted to learn how to make

things with clay. I could take pottery lessons. Yes, that's what I'll do next fall when Julie leaves." Her voice quavered as she thought about the empty house that loomed. "I'll do it. That might be fun."

* * *

All the church business that had been pushed aside for the holidays covered Suzanne's desk. Stacks of mail and catalogs sat like weights on her soul. And there was the dreaded annual statistical report to the denomination. She filled out everything she could and then called May for information about the Sunday school classes.

"Pastor Suzanne, you don't have to do that. I usually fill it out. Have you realized that our classes have been slowly increasing in attendance? Little Ella keeps bringing new friends, and we now have a family of African Americans bringing their three children to Sunday school. Their youngest boy, Dill is J's age. I'm glad for our little J. She is going to need friends of color, too, and we could all do with some broadening of our relationships. That J is quite a character. She's real active, and my but she's smart. She talks a lot, but nobody knows what she's saying. Now she's figured out how to take off the little crocheted hat Eileen puts on her every week.

"Anyway, I'll get the report filled out before our next Session meeting. Has anyone mentioned to you about another adult class?"

"No, do you mean in addition to the Bible Study?"

"Yes. Carl and Stacey and your Julie want a class about the twelve steps. I'm thinking that's a good idea. Those steps would help all of us grow even if we don't have addictions. What do you think?"

"May, that's a great idea. Have you thought about a leader?"

"Dave comes to mind, but Loretta would be excellent, too. Maybe the two of them would do it together. I'm thinking Sunday morning before church. We're almost out of room, but we could pull some chairs into the kitchen."

"Sounds good to me. You're the elder in charge of education, so go for it. I'd like to sit in on that class, too, when I can."

Chapter 24

"Let's go see if we can cheer up Melba," Suzanne said to Wolfie. "I bet she has a treat for you." The woman's whole body drooped over her desk, and she held her hand over her eyes.

"Melba, are you okay?"

"Oh, I didn't hear you coming. I'm okay, I guess, just a little headache. I never have liked January."

"How were your holidays?"

"They were okay though it's not quite right without Brenda and Pat. I can't remember when I had Christmas without them, but Billy, Norm, and I managed to put a dinner together." She took Wolfie and pulled a treat out of her bottom drawer for him. "Norm still cries about Brenda and Pat, and he keeps begging us to find them.

"Did you know we came to the Christmas Eve service? You probably didn't see us. We sat way in the back and left during the benediction. Norm doesn't want to create a fuss. It was a real nice service you had. You know, Brenda never wanted me to come to church. She said I should be the secretary for Norm and leave the rest of church things to her."

She hesitated but took a deep breath so Suzanne knew there was more to come. "I've waited to tell you until the holidays were over. But somebody's been in the church again. A whole roll of stamps is missing from my desk, and the refrigerator's been totally cleaned out. I had sandwich makings, Cokes, and apples in there. It's all gone. So I'm not feeling safe, not knowing who's getting in and how they're doing it."

Suzanne sat down. "Every church I've been in has things like this happen—except for messing with dog things. It's puzzling that someone would focus on Wolfie's treats and his carrying case. But there hasn't been any of that since I bought the little fence to use instead of a carrier. Nevertheless, you're right. It's unsettling knowing that someone's getting in. I'll talk to Dave right away. We have to be sure it's safe to work here."

* * *

Dave called her back after work and listened to Suzanne's report on the building security. "We need to think all this through again," he said. "There's something we're missing. Could you come for an early dinner tonight? I already checked with Eileen. We're having pork chops."

"Sure, I'd love to. We'll put our heads together and figure it out."

* * *

After dinner, Eileen took J to get her bath while Dave and Suzanne cleaned up and sat back down at the table with paper and pencils. Dave showed her a list of people who had keys to the new lock on the basement door. "Nobody on this list would take food from the refrigerator," he said.

"Or stamps," Suzanne added.

He showed her another list:

Ways of getting access

- *The street door*
- *Front doors*
- *Basement windows*

Suzanne rubbed her eyes. "The street door—we know everyone who has a key, and we don't leave it unlocked except on Sunday mornings."

"The front door doesn't have a key," Dave said. He stood and paced around the kitchen. "Never has. It looks like it would take an old skeleton key. I'm usually the first person here on Sunday. I come in the street door and go up to the sanctuary and unbolt that door from the inside. Every time I've checked the windows they're locked. They all stay locked, and it would take a child to climb through one, anyway."

"Could someone put tape on a lock to hold it open? I've seen that on television."

"Yes, but I've looked for signs of that," he said. "And I'm not sure when anyone would do that."

"Sunday morning when the doors are unlocked?"

"After church we pull the sanctuary doors shut. It's possible we wouldn't notice tape. But there are always lots of people standing around, so anyone we don't know would certainly stand out."

"Do the AA and NA groups still lock up during their meetings?" she asked.

"Yes, anyone who comes late can buzz to be let in. Does Melba ever leave it unlocked?"

"No, she used to when the copier was at Norm's, but we've talked through her every move during the week and mine, too. I'm stumped."

Dave sat down and tapped his pencil on the table. "What I can't figure out is why someone would bother Wolfie's carriers. It's not like they're reselling them. That first time it was in the garbage.

I can understand someone being desperately hungry and taking food from the refrigerator. Maybe even stamps if they could sell them. But why dog things?"

"Do you know of anyone who doesn't like having him here?"

"No, haven't heard a thing."

Dave reached over and tapped the list. "Rosa. She has a key. When does she clean?"

"Thursday evening."

"Has anybody told her to keep the door locked while she's here?"

"Melba talked to her. I'll double check on that. Anything else we can do?"

"Pastor, I'm going to go over this again and walk through the building once more. I'll call the man who installed the security system to see if he has any idea how someone could bypass it. One thing we could do is get the more expensive system which would give each person a code to punch in. Then we'd know who entered when."

The next day Suzanne asked Melba, "Did you tell Rosa to keep the door locked while she's cleaning?"

"Yes, she said she always does. I asked her again when I had to make a new key for her. She lost hers right after we gave everybody new ones."

"Okay. Thanks. Dave and I are still trying to figure out how someone gets in and why anyone would steal stamps and dog items. Food we can understand if someone was desperately hungry. But why take dog things and then dump them in the garbage?"

"I know. It's puzzling," she said, looking away.

* * *

Three days later when Suzanne returned from walking Wolfie, she found his little fence was missing from her office. When Melba returned from lunch, they checked every door and window for clues as to how someone had entered the building. She and Melba found the fencing behind the garbage cans. Suzanne clenched her fists. "Who's doing this?"

"Somebody must be trying to get to you," Melba said. Suzanne heard a momentary catch in her voice. "I hope they don't hurt Wolfie."

"Could it be Brenda?" she asked Melba. "Do you think she's still around here?"

Melba looked up at the sky and grimaced. "I should have told you. After I mentioned making a new key for Rosa, I remembered that I made two and put one in the back of my desk drawer 'cause you know, somebody else will lose one sooner or later. When I checked, sure enough, it was gone. But, no, I don't think it's Brenda's doing. She and Pat left town a while back."

"Right after Norm was in the hospital?"

"Soon after." She took a deep breath. "Actually, they didn't leave right away."

They stood beside the garbage cans. Suzanne didn't move a muscle, hoping Melba would go on talking.

"That first night when the police were looking for them, I brought them to the church, made dinner in the kitchen and let them sleep here. I tried to get Brenda to go to the police and clear up the misunderstanding, but she yelled at me to mind my own business. I wanted her to leave Pat with me. That girl needs to grow up. She's been tied to her mother's apron strings too long. Brenda made her into a friend instead of a daughter and made sure she was the only friend Pat had. I've never said anything about that, but when she decided to leave, I told her to leave Pat with me and Norm. Somebody had to look after him. I knew she didn't want me doing it. But she slapped me, grabbed Pat by the arm, and stalked out. The two of them left, walking south. I haven't heard from them since then.

"You have to understand. Brenda had it difficult early on, and then this with the church, with Norm asked to leave …. It's no wonder she's so upset. She's not herself."

"Do you think she has the extra key?"

"I don't think so. We had the new ones made after they left town."

"Maybe they didn't leave town, or maybe they're back."

Melba stiffened and shook her head. "They would have let me know."

* * *

Dave agreed with Suzanne. Somehow Brenda had to be behind this. Who else would take dog things and throw them away? It had to be someone wanting to irritate the pastor. He and Suzanne sat down with Rosa, and under specific questioning, she confessed to taking the extra key out of Melba's drawer because she lost another one and didn't want to tell her. She couldn't say where she lost it.

"I keep keys careful on chain and ID. So, I clip onto bucket where is supplies. I keep there so no lose. How lose twice? Chain broke? No other ones lost."

"Tell me exactly what you do when you come," Dave said. "You park near the door?"

"Yes, I park close. Take my bucket and use to hold door open. I carry supplies into church. Then I move bucket and close door. It locks."

"Is it possible you forgot to take the key from the door, and when you closed it, the key was outside?" Suzanne asked.

Rosa looked down and nodded. "One time, only one time. I found when I leave. But was only one time, and I found and …." She started to cry. "Please I need job. It never happen again. I need job. I work extra hard. Please."

Dave handed her a handkerchief. "Rosa, don't cry. You've been doing good work for us. But I think this happened more than once, and your key was taken from the door. We'll change the lock again and get new keys, but you must be more careful. Take the key from the door when you prop it open, attach it to the supply bucket before you bring it in, and be sure the door locks so you're safe inside. Let's go upstairs and I'll show you what I mean."

"I will, I will. I promise."

CHAPTER 25

SUZANNE and Julie settled into a routine at home. Together they cleaned house, did laundry, and bought groceries on Saturdays. Suzanne cooked on the weekends, making enough for several meals. Then each day Julie chose what to have for dinner, using what her mother had cooked, and had it ready when she came home. Friday night was pizza night. Matthew usually drove over from Lawrence to join them. On Sunday afternoons they had a standing date to talk with Peter.

Suzanne tried to enjoy life more, keeping two mystery novels on hand in case she finished one late at night. Life in its new chapter began to feel a bit more normal, though she often dreamed about Bell. She kept her sanity by praying for his health.

* * *

The little congregation of Lamb of God Presbyterian Church began to welcome new members, many of them as a result of Dave and Loretta inviting them. Suzanne assumed they were from their AA groups.

Suzanne told Dr. Bill, "There's a special energy in this congregation. I think it's because so many of the people know their need for God."

One day Eileen suggested to Suzanne that the church offer treats to the recovery groups that met in the church. "We used to do that a long time ago, but Brenda said it encouraged people to come just for the food." The elders on the session talked it over and approved the idea.

Loretta helped them get organized and connect with the AA and NA groups. She told Suzanne, "I don't know why we stopped. People stay around longer when there are treats, and that visiting is important. We also had a food pantry and clothing room at one time. It's a big help to folks trying to get their feet back under them and stay sober."

More activity led to more energy. And that led to more work for Suzanne. One Thursday all her plans went out the window as a result of phone calls and people dropping in. Loretta brought information about where she could take pottery classes. May had questions about a Sunday school lesson. Carl came by to thank her for taking an interest in his family and to ask for Ella to be baptized. Dave needed to talk about the next 12 step class. As a result she didn't get the information ready for Melba to type the Sunday order of worship. So she had to either come in on her day off or stay that evening until she had it all ready. If she stayed, she'd miss a presbytery committee meeting in Topeka. No good choice, she told herself, but I can't be in more than one place at a time. And I promised Dr. Bill and myself I'd stop letting work keep me from taking a day off. She stayed in the office. The title of the sermon gave her trouble. She had no idea what it would be. So she inserted the scriptures for the day and read them over again. Nothing came to her. She left the sermon title blank. *God, I'm going to have faith that you will lead me to your Word for us. And I hate to rush you, but Sunday isn't too far off, as you well know.*

She picked hymns, call to worship, confession, assurance. The rest would be as usual, and she'd work on the sermon at home. Maybe it will come to me while I'm driving, and I can still have Friday and Saturday somewhat free.

It was late. She packed her bag, woke up a sleeping Wolfie and carried him up the stairs. The wind blew the door out of her hands, and banged against the wall with a thud. Sleet pinged around her. She tucked Wolfie's head under her coat to shield him and ran for the car. As she bent over to put him in his carrier in the back seat, she heard a swish and felt pain across her shoulders which knocked her forward half in, half out of the car.

* * *

The next thing she knew lights flashed around her. She lay in an open ambulance, and a young woman held her wrist. Dave's face looked down at her. "What happened?" she asked.

"I came to open up for AA and found you knocked out cold."

"I was putting Wolfie in the car—where is he? Where's Wolfie?" She tried to raise up, but a wave of dizziness and a terrible ache on her back forced her back. The young woman gently eased her down and tightened the restraints holding her on a board.

She closed her eyes. "He's in the car. I put him in the car, in his carrier," she told Dave.

"He's not there. And I've looked all over the church. Several of the AA folks are out looking for him in the neighborhood. Don't you worry, he's around here somewhere."

"Find him." She cried uncontrollably, every sob hurting her back. "Please find him."

"Let me take care of it. He may be hiding somewhere, scared."

"No. He was in his carrier. Anyway, he would have stayed right by me. Someone's taken him."

"Was there someone here?"

"I don't know. I thought the wind blew the car door and knocked me over."

She didn't miss the look that passed between Dave and the EMT woman.

* * *

Later, she lay in the hospital, immobilized. "You mustn't move," the nurse said. "We'll be getting scans shortly to determine any damage, but until then, try to relax."

Loretta hovered by the door until the nurse left. "Suzanne, I'm so sorry. Does it hurt?"

A few minutes later Dave appeared with Julie. "Mom, Mom, are you all right?" she asked.

Peter walked in about midnight. He had borrowed his roommate's car and driven to Wichita through the sleet. "Does it hurt very bad?" he asked.

Julie held her right hand, Peter her left, and Loretta stood at the foot of the bed, squeezing her toes.

The nurse was in the process of asking them to leave when Melba crept in head down. She teared up when Dave told her there was no word about Wolfie.

"I've never seen Melba show emotion before," Dave said when the others went to the cafeteria. He walked beside her bed as a young man escorted her to radiology. "Can you think of anywhere in the neighborhood Wolfie might go?"

"No, he wouldn't have left me. Somebody has taken him." She tried to hold back the sobs, but they burst from her as though her world had ended.

CHAPTER 26

THE doctor saw her Monday morning. "You don't have a concussion, and there are no broken bones. Somebody hit you with enough force to give you whiplash, but I expect your neck to get better on its own. You must wear this collar and rest so your body can do its healing. No work for a full week."

"Doctor, my little dog is missing. I have to find him. Is it okay for me to drive?"

"Some, but I'd prefer you ride rather than drive if you absolutely have to go somewhere. I want you lying down flat on your back for at least two hours in the morning and two hours in the afternoon."

* * *

After hearing the good news, Peter drove back to college, and Dave took Julie home so she could get to classes.

By noon all the paperwork and instructions had been completed, and Loretta took charge of Suzanne. "You lie down in the back seat, and I'll avoid bumps if at all possible."

"Take me to the church. I need to get some things and look for Wolfie."

"Okay, then I'll drive you home," Loretta said.

"No. I'll need my car. Take me to the church, and I'll drive home from there. I feel pretty good."

"Suzanne, you heard what the doctor said."

"I know, but I have to do this. I'll be in the office a while, and if I don't feel like I can drive home, I'll call you. Thanks for taking care of everything."

* * *

Melba watched Loretta help Suzanne walk carefully down the stairs into the basement. "We've looked everywhere for Wolfie and put up flyers," she said through her tears. "He can't have gone far. I bet he was scared when you fell."

"Melba, I don't think he ran off. The doctor said I was hit from behind and not from the car door. I think somebody knocked me down and took him."

Melba shook her head and wiped her cheeks. "No, no, surely not."

Suzanne went to her desk and tried to sort out what was needed for the next week. Loretta filled her in. "Dave gave a talk yesterday in place of the sermon. Next Sunday I'll lead a hymn sing. I'm going to the grocery store now, but you call me. I'd feel much better if you'd let me take you home."

Loretta walked out, and Suzanne closed her eyes. Her ears rang with static, and she had to rest her chin on her palms to relieve the pain in her neck. She heard a rustle.

Melba stood at the door looking at her. Her lips tight, her fists clenched. "Come, go with me. We'll take my car. I may know what's happened."

"Brenda?"

Melba responded with a curt nod. She drove west out of Wichita, hitting every bump in the road. Suzanne clutched the door handle with one hand and held her neck with the other. She could hardly breathe. It was cold outside, but the noontime sun shone brightly, and Melba had the heat turned on high.

Outside of town most of the land was scrub grass. Here and

there cattle huddled together and blew steam clouds. Melba turned this way and that until Suzanne lost all sense of direction.

"Looks like you know this area well, Melba."

"I grew up in a town west of here, a little spot in the road now. When we were in school, Brenda, Norm, and I wandered all over this land."

She pulled down a dirt road and then turned on another. "It's a good thing we've had a couple days of dry weather after that spell of sleet. You can't hardly get back here when this clay gets wet, but the wind dries it out pretty quick."

Should I be afraid? Suzanne wondered, but remembering Melba's tears, she put those thoughts aside. Melba left the road and drove across open, rutted ground. Tumbleweeds rolled aimlessly. A rocky outcrop rose into the closest thing to a cliff in this flat land. They drove around the outcrop to where a cave had been dug out. Planks hung haphazardly across the opening. "Is this what they call a dugout?" she asked Melba.

She nodded, opening the car door. "Yes, it made for a quick shelter in the early days. Now, people are building fancy places into the sides of hills—good insulation. Wait until I motion for you to come. If I don't right away, slide down so you can't be seen."

The wind whipped and whistled around the car adding to Suzanne's anxiety. When Melba motioned to her, she carefully turned in her seat and eased her feet to the ground, then held onto the door until her dizziness passed.

Inside it was quiet—a relief from the constant wind. Suzanne followed Melba into the back to another carved out room. An old mattress lay on a wooden pallet. Someone had been there recently. An empty cracker box and Vienna sausage cans were strewn across the floor.

They looked around outside. Suzanne called, "Wolfie, Wolfie" into the wind which blew the words back to her.

"I have another idea," Melba said. "Are you able to go further?"

"Yes, yes, anything to find him." A little headache and dizziness aren't going to keep me from finding my little pup, she thought. *God, please, please help me. Let him be okay. Give me strength.*

They got back in the car, but Melba said, "You don't look so good. Wait a minute." She went around to the trunk and came back with a big bottle of water.

"Thanks. That tastes good," Suzanne said. "I'll take some aspirin." She brought her seat straight up, and put her purse behind her neck for support.

"Did you say you went to school with Brenda and Norm?"

"We grew up together, but I'm older than they are." After a long pause, Melba went on. "My dad was the local preacher, a good man, very generous. When I was fourteen and Brenda was ten, her father was killed in a bar fight. The sheriff found her locked in a closet. He brought her to our house, and Dad took her in. That's when he took my dog to a farm outside of town—she said she was allergic to it.

"She told me her dad locked her up in a closet when he went out drinking. He told her she was so ugly her mother ran off."

"That's horrible," Suzanne said. "How could someone be so ignorant?"

"That's what my daddy said, 'It's ignorance more than sinfulness.' Not sure I agree with him. I think her dad was evil. But I never said that out loud. We pretty much went along with Dad no matter what. Mother never said a word about him bringing her to live with us. Not when he brought Norm either. He came along a year after Brenda. They were the same age."

"Was Norm an orphan?"

"Yes, he appeared one day. Dad told us he needed a family. Norm remembers his parents leaving one morning and not coming back. He went to the neighbors, and they called Dad. Nobody knows if they died or just left."

"Brenda and Norm became my sister and brother. But when Mother died—I was sixteen, they were twelve—I took over and did what my mother did. We took care of people. Anyone who needed food or clothes, I'd take it to them. I never questioned it, like she didn't. I kept house, became the church secretary for my dad. I never finished school." She shook her head.

"I guess Norm finished school?"

"Yes, and the church sent him to college and seminary. He got scholarships, too. Everybody was real proud of him. Brenda and I visited him in Des Moines during seminary. That's the first time I noticed Brenda looking at him as more than a brother.

"The three of us lived together for a long time after they got married. I helped take care of Billy when he was born. But then one day Brenda told me in no uncertain terms to move into my own apartment. Still, I was always there when they needed something. We're the only family left for each other. But Brenda doesn't want anyone to know that."

"Did you know Norm was being beaten?"

"Brenda said you overreacted. Norm was fine. He didn't need to go to the hospital, and you were trying to get them out of the way by calling the police."

"Someone had beaten him."

"Are you sure?"

"Yes. Bruises all over his back. Pat said he wouldn't do what her mother told him to, that it was his fault."

"That can't be, she would nev—." Her voice faded off then came back strong. "We're going to get to the truth." She drove faster through the scrub land. Occasionally they passed a barn, a few cattle. They drove by a one-story cinderblock school whose windows were blown out and parts of the roof hung off one end of the building.

"We went to school there until the county built a big school a ways over thataway. A tornado came through here three years ago, but it was abandoned by then."

Melba gripped the steering wheel as they entered the town. It was two blocks long with a café, a trailer housing the branch of a bank, a bar, and several empty storefronts. A man sat smoking on a bench outside the post office.

The church stood at the far end of the street. Someone had spray painted X's on its faded sign. Melba pulled into the gravel driveway of the house next door. "Wait here," Melba said. She walked around the house looking in windows. They were broken out and the front door boarded up. She disappeared around back and then Suzanne could see her inside the house. She came back shaking her head and sat in the car with her eyes closed.

Backing up, she turned to go further down the road and out of town. Suzanne kept quiet. She tried to move her neck into a more comfortable position, but pain shot all the way into her eyes. She gasped.

"One more stop," Melba said. "It's not far."

I wonder how far "not far" is, Suzanne thought. She'd found that in Kansas everything was far away.

They passed a few fields of winter wheat sprouted enough to show their neat rows. More barns and a few silos appeared. Then the fields turned scrubby again. After several more miles, Melba turned down a gravel road and left onto a dirt path, stopping in front of an abandoned house. Weeds had overtaken an old well pump and the front steps. Suzanne looked out over the land. Fields stretched out for miles without any sign of other buildings. No crops grew here. No cattle were in evidence. Clumps of dead grass bent over in the wind. The house had two stories on the left half where a chimney listed to one side. On the right a one-story room leaned into the taller structure. It had a door and a window. The only tree in sight showed a lightning char which no doubt explained half of it lying on the roof, the other half looking like a finger reaching up to the sky. Melba pointed to dark clouds gathering overhead.

"I'll make this quick—doubt we'll find anything. Brenda's dad was the last person to live here as far as I know."

Suzanne got out of the car and stretched gently. Her head pounded, and she tried to remember when she'd last taken aspirin. Dare she take more? Feeling nauseous, she bent her head down between her knees.

She heard Melba stifle a scream, and she ran toward the house, nearly falling over the threshold. She heard voices. "Can you walk," Melba said to someone. Suzanne kept moving toward the back of the house, trying to see in the dark. Beyond the first room was a small kitchen. The stained sink held empty cans and a potato chip bag.

Behind the kitchen, she saw Melba leaning into a closet, trying to untie Pat. Suzanne bent to help but lost her balance and had to sit down on the floor.

The poor girl sat on a child's stool, shivering. Her feet were tied together and her arms bound behind her. Her face was pale and dirty. She smelled of urine. A bucket of water sat on another stool beside her where she could bend over and drink from it.

"There's a towel in the trunk. Get it and see if you can find anything she can wear," Melba said.

Suzanne found the towel and picked up an old bar of soap in the kitchen. She examined a sheet sitting on the floor by the sink. It was tied together by its corners. In it she found cans of vegetables and soup and candy bars. A box of dog treats sat on the floor. She explored the rest of the house calling out, "Wolfie, Wolfie." She found no sign of him.

Pat tried to talk.

"Do you need to go to the hospital?" Suzanne asked.

She coughed and choked. "No."

"Where is Wolfie?" Melba asked.

"With Mother. Takes care of an old woman."

"Can you show us where the woman lives?"

"No. Mom locked me up when I tried to get away."

"Just like her dad did to her in that house," Melba mumbled. "Just like her dad. She's gone completely off her rocker."

Once Melba had Pat cleaned up, she tied the sheet around her like a toga, threw her own coat over her and carried her to the car. Suzanne slid in first, and they helped Pat lie down on the back seat with her head in Suzanne's lap.

Suzanne brushed Pat's hair back from her face. "Pat, you probably don't know that Billy's back. He and your dad are living together," Suzanne said.

"Billy? He's dead."

Suzanne took her hand. "Turns out he's not. He looks good."

Melba sprinted back to Wichita, outracing the clouds and getting to Norm's house as a cold rain started. Suzanne had fallen asleep, one hand behind her neck and the other holding Pat's hand. Both woke when the car stopped.

Melba said, "Pat, you don't have any broken bones. I figure with some food and rest, you'll be okay until we can get you to the doctor tomorrow. But if you want me to I'll take you to the emergency room tonight. Either way, I think Suzanne needs to lay down right now. Wait here. I'll get help."

Suzanne stayed where she was, uncertain how much it would hurt if she tried to get up. Pat stayed put, too, until they heard Billy's footsteps.

"Pat, Suzanne, I'm coming. We'll get you out of here."

Pat cried and moaned when he lifted her like a baby and carried her in the house. Suzanne tried to get up, but then Melba was there lifting her shoulders, holding her head steady, and Billy returned to carry her in and lay her on the couch. Norm put a pillow under her head and pulled an afghan over her.

Pat sat opposite her in a chair sobbing between hiccups. "I thought you were dead," she said to Billy.

"I almost was but now I'm here. We'll have lots of time to talk. Right now let's get you some food and water."

Norm brought in a blanket to cover her. "Buddy's here. Now we need to get Mother back," he said.

Melba brought in bowls of soup. She handed one to Suzanne and sat by Pat, feeding her a spoonful at a time. "Not too much at once," she said.

As she ate her soup, Suzanne watched what was left of that family, torn apart and in shreds, yet taking care of each other.

The back door slammed, and Loretta marched in. "Has anyone seen Suzanne?" She stopped at the doorway to the living room. "What's going on? Pat! Are you okay?"

"She's had a traumatic time," Suzanne said. "Melba and I found her in an old house where Brenda used to live when she was a child."

"Lord, have mercy," Loretta said moving to Pat's side and gingerly hugging her. "And you." She turned to Suzanne. "You're supposed to be home resting. What happened?"

"Melba had an idea where Wolfie might be, so we went looking. And we found Pat, thank God."

"Wolfie's with Brenda somewhere," Melba said.

Billy brought in chairs from the kitchen, but before Loretta could sit down, there was another slam of the back door.

"Where's that no good, ugly daughter of mine?"

Dishes crashed. A dog yipped.

"Wolfie?" Suzanne whispered.

Norm moved quickly. "Brenda," he called out. "We're in here."

She appeared in the doorway with a bat in one hand. With the other arm, she held Wolfie. She swung at Norm, catching his wrists as he held out his arms to her. Wolfie had a rope around his neck. Brenda held him tightly, almost choking him. Suzanne tried to get up, but dizziness clouded her eyes and her stomach threatened to give back the soup. She sank back onto the couch, then tried again. She had to get to Wolfie.

"Mom, give me the bat," Billy said holding his hand out.

"I'm not your mother," she said, swinging at him. "You shoulda stayed dead. And you—" She glared at Pat. "You shoulda stayed where I put you. If you did what you were told, and if you weren't so ugly, your dad wouldn't have made such a mess of things."

Pat cowered into the chair and put a pillow over her face.

Billy said, "Mother, you're not making sense."

Melba crept up beside her. "Brenda, calm down, and let's talk about this."

Brenda pointed the bat at her. "You shut up. Stay out of my business. Always interfering, thinking you're better than me."

When Brenda focused on Melba, Suzanne quickly grabbed for Wolfie. "Mind your own business, Bitch," Brenda shouted jerking him away. "This is all your fault." Suzanne feared she would choke him. He was slipping further from her left arm, and she kept tightening her grip around his neck. Suzanne reached again, but Brenda swung the bat with one hand like she was hitting a baseball. It would have crushed Suzanne's head, but Loretta pulled her back in time. A lamp crashed to the floor. The bat hit the wall. Billy jumped. He grabbed the bat and threw it down the hall. Melba pulled Wolfie away. Billy held his mother in an awkward embrace.

"Let me go," Brenda yelled. "You shit-faced asshole. Stop touching me. You're going to hell, all of you. The sooner the better." She struggled, but Billy held on and with Loretta's help took her outside. Melba called 911.

Norm sat on the arm of Pat's chair. His wrists lay limply in his lap.

Suzanne took her little dog from Melba, untied the rope around his neck, and checked for injuries. Finding none, she sat down and let him lap up the remaining soup from her bowl.

Melba knelt down in front of them. "Poor, little Wolfie. I wonder if this trauma will stay with him."

"I was wondering that, too." Suzanne said. "But maybe dogs don't hold onto such things."

* * *

Flashing lights, sirens, police cars, an ambulance. Questions. Tears. They all gathered outside. Brenda glared at Norm, her teeth bared like a wild animal. He still looked puzzled as a paramedic wrapped his wrists and took him off to the hospital.

When the cold rain turned to sleet again, they left Brenda with the police and went back inside. Loretta phoned Julie, who had called her earlier, in tears, saying her mother hadn't arrived home. She called Dave, too. Finally the police said Suzanne could leave. Loretta ordered her to lie down in the back seat. She would drive her home. Dave would follow in Suzanne's car.

* * *

She slept off and on in the back seat with Wolfie in one of her arms while the other arm and hand supported her neck trying to find a position that didn't hurt. At home, Dave helped her into the house and up the stairs. Julie had her gown and robe laid out on her bed. She also had placed a box of chocolates, her mystery novels, and an automatic teapot on the bedside table.

"We've all agreed you will take a mandatory two weeks sick leave," Dave said. "So then you'll be back for Ash Wednesday and the beginning of Lent."

"Stay in bed as much as possible," Loretta ordered.

Julie kissed her forehead. "I'll take care of you and Wolfie."

CHAPTER 27

By the time Suzanne returned to work, the excitement had died down. *I should have been here to help them through this time of upset within the congregation,* she thought as she drove the familiar roads. *What are they thinking about Brenda? How will this affect their relationships with each other? With God?*

I have a lot to talk with Dr. Bill about, she thought. *He doesn't know about my injury. He doesn't know I almost lost Wolfie.*

Melba met her at the bottom of the steps into the fellowship hall and office area. She took Wolfie from her arms and hugged him. "I'm so glad you're back. Loretta has kept us informed, and we're all relieved you're okay. And here you are, little Wolf babe. I promised Billy you'd come over there as soon as possible."

"How are they?"

"They're doing pretty well. I've been cooking dinner for them every night."

After checking messages and finding nothing urgent, she and Wolfie walked next door. From the side entrance, she saw Billy in the kitchen. He waved her in. After drying his hands, he gave her a big hug and picked up Wolfie. "I know somebody who wants to see you," he said.

In the living room Pat and Norm sat in front of the television. Norm's arms were still bandaged. Both jumped up when they saw her. "You're back! Are you okay?" Norm said.

"We're fine," she said, hugging both of them. At first Pat stiffened, but then lightly hugged back.

While the men cooed over the dog, Suzanne whispered to Pat, "How are you?" Pat avoided her eyes.

"Okay."

Suzanne sat down. "Pat, I really want to know how you are. And I want to know how your mother is."

Pat glanced up, but said nothing.

Billy sat the dog next to Norm on the couch and moved to Pat's chair. "You have something you want to say to Pastor Suzanne?"

"Thank you," she said.

Billy put his arm around Pat. "We're all thankful for what you and Melba did."

"I'm glad you're okay and me, too, but tell me what happened to your mother."

"She was taken to the hospital and evaluated. Now she's in a ...." He looked down at Pat who had collapsed back into her chair. "A facility, a secure medical facility where she's getting all the help available. She's ill."

Norm chattered at Wolfie in the background while Billy and Suzanne sat looking at Pat, waiting for her to say something. Finally, she did. "She's ill ... and she's evil." She sobbed. "She told me you were dead. I missed you so much."

Billy knelt down by her chair and held her hand.

* * *

Several people stopped by the church office in the afternoon. Eileen brought a cooler of food. Little J squealed with joy when Wolfie took a treat from her hand.

Later, Suzanne heard Loretta's high heels on the steps and hurried out of her office to see her. She handed a big bouquet of tulips to Suzanne. "It's spring in Mexico!" she said. "And it will be coming here before you know it. Now, tell me, are you glad to see us, or were you having too much fun at home?"

Suzanne laughed. "Bored, I was getting so bored." She winked. "But I did enjoy sleeping in every morning. Come, sit down. Let's have a cup of tea and put these flowers where we can enjoy them. I have questions."

In her office with only Wolfie to hear the conversation, Suzanne asked, "What is the mood of the congregation? I've missed a lot of Sundays, two when Bell left and now two more. Is there any talk about that?"

"Sure, but most of the talk is concern about you and Pat. Only one person questioned how much sick leave you had. We made clear announcements in church both Sundays. Your injuries were job related, and the session was fully supportive of watching out for your health. Dave said, 'Our pastor is always here for us. Now, we're here for her.' There was a spontaneous cheer from the congregation. Took us all by surprise. Now, Dave will be here in a few minutes. We have something to talk to you about." Suzanne stiffened. "Now, don't worry, honey. It's all good."

* * *

Dave came in looking serious. They're dismissing me with thanks, she thought. My interim year is up pretty soon anyway. They're probably in good enough shape to look for a pastor. I'd better start looking for another church. We can't miss even one week of a salary.

"We did pretty well on our own, Pastor. It's one thing we appreciate about you. You let us do things, and they don't have to be perfect. I talked about the twelve steps the first Sunday morning, and Loretta led a hymn sing yesterday. But, don't get me wrong. We're glad you're back. We need you."

He cleared his throat. "Pastor, the session asked Loretta and me to talk with you. We appreciate all you've done for this congregation since you've been here. Attendance is up, we have two new adult classes and three for the children. We have four women involved in providing treats for the AA meetings, and they're also talking about starting food pantry. Carl's been talking to some people from other churches about starting a clothing room together."

"Worship is exciting. Your pastoral care is outstanding. I don't know how you keep up with the hospitals and nursing homes and still visit the shut-ins regularly."

Dave cleared his throat again. Okay, Suzanne thought, now for the real thing. "The Moderator of the Committee on Ministry called me, and I had a conversation with the Presbytery executive, also. They want us to prepare a Mission Study to state as clearly as we can what we see as our ministries now and in the future."

Loretta added, "I feel like we're just now waking up."

Suzanne wasn't prepared for this, not today. She had looked forward to seeing her people after two weeks away. Their faces flashed through her mind: The congregation singing the old gospel songs, clapping and beaming; Loretta in her western bling leading them; Wolfie sitting with the children during their special time; the colors of people now matching more closely the population of the neighborhood around them; Eileen and Dave with little J standing on the pew between them, holding onto their shoulders; Carl and Stacey in the front pew; Ella in the back of the church passing notes with her pre-teen friends; May and the older women huddled together in their pew, dreaming dreams for the children; and her own Peter and Julie welcomed by this church family.

Wolfie walked over to Dave and stood on his hind legs asking to be picked up. Dave held the dog on his lap while explaining that he knew an interim could only stay a short time, and they wished it weren't so. "I told the Presbytery folks we need you for another year, and if there's any way it can happen, we'd like to have you stay even longer than that. They said another year is fine with them, but for now I—we need to know if you'd consider staying past the May 1 date. Would you stay with us another year or even six months if a year's too much to ask?"

She took a deep breath. "Yes, yes. I'd like to." She caught herself: I don't know if they need me, but I sure need them. But remember, she told herself, this is not about you, it's about what this congregation needs. She thought a moment. "I agree with you. I think it's in the best interest of this congregation to take another year to get settled enough to call a pastor."

"Good, good," he said.

"That's not all," Loretta added. "We've voted a raise for you. Our budget is healthy for the first time since I don't know when. You've been exactly what we needed. We think you deserve an increase. And Sunday dinners at my house are included."

Dave turned the little dog to look him in the eyes. "Wolfie, will you be our church dog for another year?" The pup nuzzled under his chin. "Good enough answer for me," he said.

Made in the USA
Charleston, SC
08 April 2016